solo

By *New York Times* Bestselling Author

kwame alexander

with Mary Rand Hess

BLINK

BLINK

Solo
Copyright © 2017 by Kwame Alexander

This title is also available as a Blink ebook.

Requests for information should be addressed to:
Blink, 3900 Sparks Drive SE, Grand Rapids, Michigan 49546

Hardcover ISBN 978–0–310–76183–9

ITPE ISBN 978–0–310–76184–6

Barnes and Noble edition ISBN 978–0–310–62848–4

Target edition ISBN 978–0–310–62840–8

Scholastic edition ISBN 978–0–310–09159–2

Cover design: Micah Kandros Design
Interior design: Denise Froehlich

Printed in the United States of America

17 18 19 20 21 22 23 24 25 /LSC/ 18 17 16 15 14 13 12 11 10 9 8 7 6 5 4 3 2 1

For my wife, Stephanie, because you love me —KA

For Garrett and the boys —MRH

Part One:

Hollywood

There's this dream

I've been having
about my mother
that scares
the holy night
out of me,
and each time I wake
from it
I'm afraid to open
my eyes
and face
the world that awaits, the
fractured world
that used to make sense,
but now seems
disjointed—islands of possibility
that float by—like
a thousand puzzle pieces
that just don't fit
together anymore.

So I think
of Chapel
and grab hold
of the only other thing
that matters.
My guitar.

Strings

Mom used to play
this game
on the tour bus
to help us
go to sleep:

Who's the best?

We'd go through
every instrument:
piano, drums, horns.
Our favorite was guitar.

My sister, Storm, always said
Eddie Van Halen
was her favorite,
probably 'cause

he once made her
pancakes
at 4 am
in a Marriott kitchen.

Ask Rutherford and
he'd say,
I'm the best in the world,
I'm outta this world.
Electric soul brother interstellar man,
which is ironic
because he was trying
to quote
Lenny Kravitz, who

Mom would say
was in her top three
along with Jimi Hendrix
and me,
just to piss him off.

Chapel

is the great song
in my life.
The sweet arpeggio
in my solo.

Her lines bring
color and verve
to my otherwise
crazy life.

Without her
I'd be a one-man band,
with a played-out sound
and no audience.

The magic
we compose
is endless,
immortal.

We could play
together
for centuries.
If I'm lucky.

And I love
the music
our bodies
make
when we're dancing.

But there is one thing
about my girlfriend
I don't understand.
She says

she doesn't believe
in sex
before marriage,
but she never

wants to get married.
When I ask her, Where is this all going, then?
she likes to
get real close,

eyelash close,
and say things like
Let's live in the moment, babe
or *we don't need labels,*

and then
she kisses me
like we own the world
and nothing else matters.

It's funny how
going nowhere
feels like it's
going someplace

fast.

Texts from Chapel

7:37 pm
On your way stop by
Best Buy pls. Headphones broke.
Red or purple. K?

7:47 pm
They finally left. I
hate hiding. Wish my dad
wasn't so CRAY. He

7:48 pm
thinks all the things
the tabloids say
about your family

7:48 pm
are true. He doesn't know
you're different, Blade.
He says

7:48 pm
you're going to
drag me into sex
and drugs.

7:49 pm
Hurry up and get here.
They're at Bible study
'til 10 . . .

Leaving in ten minutes

Sorry. Working on a song.
Beats or *Bose*?
And tell the Reverend I
only did drugs once.

The Show

My father,
Rutherford Morrison,
can't stand
to be away
from the stage.
He has always craved
the spotlight,
needs it
like a drug,
posing, posturing, profiling
before millions—
an electric prophet, or so he thinks,
capturing concert worshipers
in the vapors
of his breath,
as if his voice
was preparing them
for rapture.

My sister and I
have always lived
under the stage,
beside it,
behind it.

The After-Party

There was always
another party.
More loud music.
More loud groupies.
Booze
and still more groupies.

I was nine.

He grabbed me
and held
a sizzling cig
in front
of my face.
Only it wasn't a cig.
He blew smoke
circles around me
and laughed.
My boy.

The band uncles got
in on the joke too,
and I stuck my tongue
in a shot glass
full of whiskey,
soaked it up
like a dirty sponge.
I loved making them laugh.

The whiskey hurt
my throat and
stung my eyes.
But the laughs
were epic.

Before I knew it

I was taking my finger
and dragging it
across powdered
sugar that looked
like ant snow trails
on the table.
Rutherford was too busy
kissing his ego
to notice.
I tasted it once,
twice, and
a few more times,
trying to find
that sugar sweet.

But, it wasn't sweet.
It was salty
bitter
and it coated
my mouth
in numbness.

I woke up
in the ICU
frightened
and embarrassed
by my father,
who sat by
my bedside
crying
in handcuffs.

Hollywood Report

Rutherford Morrison has kept rock alive for twenty-five years.
His band, The Great Whatever, is credited with introducing a new flavor of

Hard Rock to America with the release of their triple-platinum album,
The History of Headaches. Even after an acrimonious band breakup,

Morrison continued to have an illustrious solo career, selling thirty million albums worldwide.

His music has lasted the test of time . . . until now.
Eight years ago, he was arrested for reckless endangerment of his child,

and he hasn't released an album since.
Most recently he's managed three DUIs, and a drug overdose

that almost sent him to a rock-star reunion with Kurt Cobain and Amy Winehouse.

Rutherford may not have much time left before he falls flat on 12:00. Midnight can be so cruel.

Who doesn't feel sorry for his kids,
left answering the hard questions, like

How does it feel
to be the daughter
to be the son
of a fallen rock star?

Who Am I?

I am
the wretched son
of a poor
rich man.

I do not hate
my life.

I am not like
Sebastian Carter,
who found
his father kissing
his girlfriend

and now hates
his life.

My life is, hmmm,
inconvenient.

But
if it weren't for Chapel . . .

Are You Sure They Aren't Coming Home?

Chapel and I are about to take flight,
two souls on fire

burning through sacred mounds of
fresh desire.

Our lips are in the process
of becoming

one
in her hammock,

like two blue jays nesting.
Feeding each other

kisses of wonder.
I'm sure, she answers.

Hands of curiosity.
What are you doing?

Kissing you.
Slow down, Blade.

Why?
Woo me.

Woo you?
A song.

Come on, babe, we don't have time for that.
But we have time for this? she says,

puckering her lips, and
hypnotizing me

with eyes blue
as the deep blue sea.

Those Eyes Will Be the Death of Me

My gravestone will read:
Here lies a young man
who died inside
the gaze of a woman.

I watch the river
in her eyes gallop forth
fall into them
dive into them.

She smiles.
Those eyes.
I can't escape
the depth of them.

The song has ended,
but the melody still rings
from her mouth.
I can't hear a word.

I'm lost
in these two comets
that move across
my universe.

I remember
the first time
she looked at me
like this.

Two years ago

before he hit
an all-time low,
Rutherford threw
one of his

Hollywood Rocker House Parties
which became Storm's
pool party
SLASH sweet sixteen
SLASH get-all-the-kids-at-our-school-drunk-so-they-
could-listen-to-Storm's-mixtape-and-think-it-is-hot
party.

While they dove deep
in shallowness,
I found a quiet corner,
a vintage Rutherford Morrison guitar
took it off the wall
and started playing
American Woman
and any tune
with a hard groove
to soften
the dull.

Minutes
or an hour
went by
before I looked up,
and there she was
sitting
in the chair
across from me,
her legs

with dancer calves
entwined
like twin yellow flowers.
Her skin, amber sun.
And those pretty blue eyes
just watching me
like she cared.

Amazing. Keep playing, she said. *Don't let me interrupt
you.* And
then she got up,
sauntered off
glancing over her shoulder,
leaving me
thunderstruck.

Those eyes.
Those blue eyes.

Later, I bumped into Storm

in the kitchen,
making grapefruit
and vodka smoothies
for her already drunk friends,
and she introduced me
to the new girl
in school.

Those eyes.

*My name's Chapel, but you can call me American
Woman*, she said, winking
at me.

Your brother's a musical genius, she continued, at which
Storm laughed.
Yeah, he's a legend in his own mind!

Chapel winked
at me again,
and just as I was
about to turn
and leave,
she reached
in my pocket,
grabbed my phone,
and took a selfie
then texted
herself
the photo.

That was the moment
I knew.

And I stayed up
all night
writing a song
about it.

Trance

Well?
Huh?

Where'd you go?
Just thinking.

About what?
I don't know—everything, graduation, family. I'm just worried.

Family sucks.
So true.

Is he coming to graduation?
Yep. He says he's been clean for nine days.

That's great.
Yup.

Tomorrow, this time, you'll be a college freshman.
Actually, I'll be in-between. No longer high school, not yet college.

No longer, not yet.
At least we'll be together every day then.

You'll have me whenever you want.
That's why I love you.

Okay then, sing my favorite song, please.
Chapel, I really don't feel like—

Blade, are you my heart?
Uh, yeah!

Then sing to me . . . Van would have.
Let's not talk about your untalented, nefarious, wack ex-lover.

Chambers

if I am your *heart*
imagine me inside
beating, pumping, loving

Relentless

Don't haiku me, Blade. I want an epic.
I don't have my guitar.

You always have your guitar.
It's in the car, but I—

I'll get it, she interrupts, jumping
off the hammock so fast,

I tumble and eat dirt.

Excuse Me

Excuse me
I mean, what did you say?
I'm sorry
I'm just a little blown away

'Cause your eyes . . . Oh, your eyes.

Excuse me,
Didn't quite get that
You talking to me?
I just gotta get my breath

'Cause your eyes . . .
Your eyes, they mesmerize me
Yes, your eyes hypnotize me
Your eyes are . . .
Bluer than the deepest part of the deep blue sea

Excuse me
I don't mean to intrude
I'm sorry
Your eyes are too blue
Forgive me
I just wanted to be sure
Your eyes, that shade.
Isn't that what they call azure?

'Cause your eyes . . .
Your eyes, they mesmerize me
Yes, your eyes hypnotize me
Your eyes are . . .
Bluer than the deepest part of the deep blue sea

I'm sorry
I don't wanna take your time
I have to say this
And I hope that you don't mind

Your eyes, they mesmerize me
Yes, your eyes hypnotize me
Your eyes are . . .
Bluer than the deepest part of the deep blue sea

Excuse me
I don't mean to intrude
I'm sorry
Your eyes are too blue
Forgive me
I just wanted to be sure
Your eyes, that shade,
Don't they call that azure?

'Cause your eyes are mesmerizing
Your eyes are hypnotizing,
Your eyes are truly drowning me
I'm drowning in a blue that's way bluer than the
    deep blue sea

'Cause your eyes . . .
Your eyes are mesmerizing
Your eyes are hypnotizing
Your eyes are drawing me to you

© BLADE MORRISON

She Melts Right in Front of Me

That was beautiful.
Thanks.

It really makes me feel special when you play for me.
You are special.

Here's your phone. Come kiss me.
What are you doing with my phone?

You left it in your car.
Oh. Thanks.

Why is Principal Campbell blowing your phone up?
Huh?

Come here, babe.
Let me ask you a question.

Enough talking. Hurry up and kiss me. They'll be home soon.
Aren't you sick of sneaking around?

The alternative sucks.
True.

We should just run away.
I would do that in an LA second. I love you, Chapel.

Then come over here and let me mesmerize you.
First, let me check my phone. Dude left me like five messages.

Seriously, Blade. Now you're all patient.
Just gimme a sec.

Voice Mail

Blade, this is
Principal Campbell calling
you about twelve hours
before you march
across the stage.
Congratulations!
You've overcome
some serious odds,
and I'm sure
your family is proud.
So, I'm calling because
I'm afraid that
our valedictorian
Alice Johnson
has been bitten
by a mosquito,
and her face
has blown up
the size of
a cantaloupe.
Thusly, she refuses
to stand
in front of
the graduating class
and their families
to deliver
tomorrow's commencement speech,
which means
the salutatorian
will have to fill in.

What do you say?

Salutatory

Blade! WHAT? You're going to deliver the speech! I'm so proud of you. Of us.
Of what? I haven't written anything yet. So don't be too proud.

You'll be amazing.
Not if I don't get home and write the thing.

Stay here with me. I can help you.
Write an entire speech before your parents find us? Not likely.

Who says it has to be a speech. It could be a song.
Hmmm. That might be cool.

You could write one about me.

. . . .

(I laugh.)
(She pouts.)

I'm serious.
Babe, it may not be the audience for that kind of love song.

But it would be the most romantic thing you've ever done for me. And people would be talking about it for months.

Let me think about it. But first, I should really get home and actually write it.
Fine.

Just know I won't sleep one millisecond tonight because I'll be thinking about you the entire time, Chapel.
Okay. Make us all want to sing with you, babe.

I grab
my guitar

and kiss her
goodbye.

Tell your dad to pray for the salutatorian, just don't
mention his name.

I wonder if anyone has

ever delivered
a graduation speech with
a six-string guitar?

Close One

I pull out of
the driveway,
onto the street,
and duck
as far
as I can
'til I'm barely able
to see
her father's black Mercedes
turn the corner
and pull into
the driveway.

Whew, that was a close one.

Secret

Chapel's father
forbade her
to see me
after Rutherford
got arrested
again
last year,
for crashing
into a stop sign
inches away
from two kids
crossing the street.
He was lit
and careless
and it was all over
the news.

He is runnin' with the devil.
They will destroy themselves.
They will not destroy you.
This is not up for discussion.
You. Are. Never. To See. Him. Again.

And so we sneak.

I Can't Say I Blame Him

My family
stands for
too much
and not enough.

Too much celebrity
not enough dignity.
Too much excess
not enough kindness.

Too much Yes.
Not enough No
to drugs
to crude behavior
to breaking the law
to rock & roll.

Too much.
Not enough.

So yeah . . .
we sneak.

Texts to Chapel

10:32 pm
I made it home.
Just hours
to spare before

10:32 pm
I either nail it or
embarrass myself to death
and walk off the stage

10:32 pm
never to show
my face again.
But it's just a song, right?

10:33 pm
Can you believe
it's almost our
big day?

10:35 pm
I know I won't
get to see you except
from a distance.

10:36 pm
But I'll look for you

10:36 pm
from the stage
when I perform
a song about

10:36 pm
how we are the chords
that make music
the language of love.

Conversation

Blade, whatcha doing?
Does anyone knock anymore?

*An open door is an open invitation. Sounds like you're
struggling.*
I am. Writing a song for graduation tomorrow.

I heard. Congratulations, little bro. How's it coming?
It's not.

You could write about love.
Everybody wants me to write about *love*.

You and love songs go together like Mick and Jagger.
You're stupid.

I'm serious. Write a love song.
I need some inspiration.

What about Mom?
What about her?

Maybe you could write a love song about her.
. . . .

But not on that busted guitar, get the one Dad gave you.

The Bridge

Rutherford gave it to me
in grand fashion
on a black velvet bench
for my thirteenth birthday—
a custom-built
Eddie Van Halen
Frankenstrat,
made of
body—ash
neck—maple,
with pickups tweaked
by EVH himself.

Legend has it
that Eddie was gonna give it
to some king
in Africa or something,
but my dad convinced him
to gift it to me.

And that's real cool,
I get it, but
what mattered
to me
was that when I strummed,
it sounded
like Mom
laughing.

So I named her Sunny,
after my mother.
And there hasn't been a day,
no matter how crazy
or wicked

or cruel,
that I haven't held her
knowing it's
the bridge
that connects
heaven
and earth.

In my house

guitars
are the holy grail,
the keepers

of our secrets
and our prayers,
but tonight God's

not on my side,
'cause I can't write
a lick,

and the whole world's
gonna know
real soon.

While I'm in

my room
swimming
in a fishbowl,
trying to write
my life
on strings,
I hear loud talking
and laughter
downstairs.

At 3 am.

Uncle Stevie

who used to play
drums
in my dad's band,
is in the foyer
smoking
dressed like
he's about to
Rock the Casbah—leather
pants, leather jacket,
Ray-Bans, and worn
snakeskin shoes.

Somebody forgot to tell you, the eighties left, I say.
C'mere, you little bugger, he says, grabbing me in a
headlock.

*Blade, why aren't you asleep? You need your rest for
tomorrow.*
I could ask you two the same question.

Kid, we haven't slept in thirty years.
Party like rock stars, huh?

We're just two dudes riding the elevator to heaven.
No stairway, huh?

Too old for stairs, kid.
Speak for yourself, Stevie.

What are you doing up?
I'm still writing, y'all wanna help?

We'd, uh, love to, kid, but we got some business.
What kind of business?

They look
at each other

as if they've stolen
the last cookie
in the jar.

We're just going to grab some coffee and talk, Rutherford
says.
You think I'm stupid enough to fall for that story again?
We've been doing THIS for years.

He's right, it's only coffee. I haven't imbibed in nine days.
Your dad's clean, Blade. We're talking about getting the
band back together. That's all, I promise, kid.

Stevie, we can't leave this amateur here by himself trying
to craft a masterpiece. Let's show him how we make magic,
then we have our breakfast meeting.
Then you show up at my graduation.

Then we show up at your graduation.
Okay.

Cool, now show us what you got written so far, kid.
Well, right now, it's mainly an, uh, idea.

You got nothing?
I got nothing.

For all his flaws

Rutherford
is Picasso
with pen and guitar.

This could be
the first graduation speech
to win a Grammy.

Even though he writes
life's woes and wonders
like a *boss*,

he hasn't been able
to right *his* life
since October 10, 2007.

October 10, 2007

Storm was in the pool
or getting her nails painted paisley,
and Mom was asleep.

She was tired of The Road.
She wanted to be home.
We all did.

Except Rutherford.
He and his band
The Great Whatever

were in Vegas
for the third
sold-out concert.

He promised
Sunny, this is the last one.
But, he'd said that before.

I begged her
to let me
go to the concert.

No, I'm feeling lucky,
she said. *Do you know
what today is?*

It's 10/10.
What does that mean?
No idea, but maybe

it'll bring us
some luck.
Let's go play

the slots. So when he left
for sound check

we left
the penthouse too
in our own

private elevator
that went straight
to the casino.

Between
our floor—thirty-five—and
the lobby,

the display read:
E Z.
Mom and I took turns

trying to figure it out.
Emotional Zebra.
Nice one, Mom.

She dropped one coin
and then another
into the first slot.

Expressionless Zombie.
Entry Zone.
Egalitarian Zealot.

YEAH! she said,
laughing so hard
she didn't even notice

she'd won
$190
in the quarter slots.

Then we walked
outside the Bellagio
and headed downtown.

You take half, she said
handing me a wad
of bills.

We stopped
at Magic Marley's music store
and I bought

*Track by Track: The Greatest Songs You Must Hear Before
You Die*
a thousand pages
that cost most

of my winnings.
Good choice, she said, smiling.
You're a star in the making, Blade.

On the way back, near
the hotel,
she stopped to smell

some yellow flowers
then bit a piece of one.
Seriously, Mom?

What? Marigold. Edible Zest.
Yeah, for a bee.
Watch out, Mom.

MOM, WATCH OUT!
But it was too late.
She got stung.

*Too sweet
for my own good,* she said
laughing, and

rubbing the bump
swelling
on her neck.

50

Evil Zapper, she said
laughing again.
We walked inside

the lobby,
but never made it
to the elevator

because she
fell to the ground
right beneath

the famous
glass sculpture.
The doctor said

an allergic reaction
to the bee sting
triggered

a brain aneurysm.
She died.
Right there

in the casino lobby
while The Great Whatever
rocked the stage.

That was ten years ago.
Rutherford never forgave himself.
And his life spiraled

into a quicksand of
nothingness.
Empty Zeroness.

Track 1: Thinking of You

ROCKER: LENNY KRAVITZ / ALBUM: *5* / LABEL: *VIRGIN AMERICA* /
RECORDING DATE: 1998 / STUDIO: COMPASS POINT STUDIOS IN THE
BAHAMAS

While we're writing
the song
that I'm to play
in less than nine hours
in front of
three thousand people,
the song
that I've decided
to dedicate
to my mom,
Uncle Stevie plays
some Lenny
for inspiration,
then explains
that most people
only know that
Lenny wrote
it about his mother,
but no one knows
that she was
an actress
on a sitcom
called The Jeffersons
or that
one of his bandmates
actually played
Heineken bottles
on the track,
which would be

52

a pretty cool story
if I hadn't heard him
tell it
a million times.

My dad
jets for the pool
and a cig
because
the song
makes him
think
of her.

The song's a hit! Went for coffee. Break a leg, killer!

I doze off
a few hours later
and wake up
to Rutherford's red Maserati
making skid marks
down our driveway
and a note
on my mirror.

Graduation Day

From the stage
I see Chapel
blow me a kiss.

I get so lost
in her deep blues
I almost don't hear

Principal Campbell
introduce
Our salutatorian,

Blade Morrison.

Climbing the Steps to Speak

I throw
　my guitar
　　over my
　　　shoulder and
　　　walk to
　　　　center stage
　　　　and start
　　　　　strumming to
　　　　　　loud applause
　　　　　but I
　　　　　　never get
　　　　　　to sing
　　　　　　　because
　　　　　　　I realize
　　　　　　　　they're not
　　　　　　　clapping
　　　　　　　　for me.

On the biggest stage of my life

in the middle
of the most important thing
I've ever done
a woman wearing
a black helmet,
matching bikini,
and nothing else
rides a red Harley
onto the football field
with a man
in the same outfit
holding a guitar
high above his head
screaming
I LOVE ROCK 'N' ROLL!

I stare in disbelief
and shame
at Chapel
at Principal Campbell
at the graduating class
egging him on
with cheers
and roars
even after
the bike slams
into the front
of the stage
and he gets up
steps on
the biker woman
then stumbles
his way

up the steps
to the mic
to me.

Rock and Roll, Blade, my father whispers
hugging me
with breath
that smells like
the devil's mouthwash.

My father

has a map
on his body that tells you
everything you don't
want to know about him.

A sun on his right shoulder.
A storm cloud with a bolt of lightning on his left.
A blade running down the back of his neck.
Over his heart: STILL HERE.

But, we're not. Still. Here.
This is the end of the road.
While he bares his wretched self
in front of the world

I walk off stage
to the sound
of his vomiting
and cell phones clicking.

I'm not even mad.
I'm just done.
Being here.
Being a Morrison.

Texts from Chapel after Graduation

9:08 pm
*I'm sorry I couldn't
be there
to comfort you.*

9:08 pm
*Parents.
Grandparents.
Graduation dinner.*

9:09 pm
*My parents made a point
NOT to talk about
you or what happened.*

9:09 pm
*I was sad and on
the verge of tears
the whole time at dinner.*

9:10 pm
*I kept thinking
about you and how
embarrassed you must be.*

9:10 pm
*I bet your song
was DOPE though.
Play it for me later?*

Hollywood Report

Rock & Roll Royalty has proven yet again
that no one knows how to screw up bigger

and better than Rutherford Morrison.
Just yesterday, he crashed his son's

graduation ceremony, literally,
drunk driving into the stage

moments before Blade Morrison was to deliver
the commencement address. Thankfully, no one was
injured,

except the already damaged ego and reputation
of his only son.

Rumor has it that Rutherford had been sober
for a short period of time, nine days, but who's counting.

According to reports, he's headed back to rehab,
for the ninth time in as many years, but again who's
counting?

As much as we all still love his music,
if rehab doesn't work, jail or death might be the only fix.

Track 2: When the Lights Go Out

ROCKERS: THE BLACK KEYS / ALBUM: *RUBBER FACTORY* / LABEL:
BLACK POSSUM RECORDS / RECORDING DATE: JANUARY–MAY,
2004 / STUDIO: AN ABANDONED TIRE MANUFACTURING FACTORY IN
AKRON, OHIO

I try reading   it doesn't help
I try strumming   it doesn't help
I try eating   it doesn't help

So I just lay here
with the lights out
listening to The Black Keys.

Staring into
the desolation
of my brokenness.

Eventually falling
into a sea
of dreams

drowning
in the dark
deep beneath

the place
where dreams
have no rules.

Dream Variation: Spin a Song

In the dining room
Rutherford
sits
at the opposite end
of the Italian marble table.
(Even our dreams are excess.)

Atop the table
is a feast
of desserts—my favorites:
red velvet Oreos
red velvet cupcakes
red everything—including
a garden of red roses
(each with the initial **BU**
tattooed on them).

Bumpy Umbrella, Rutherford says
matter-of-factly,
with the sincerest grin
aimed at my mother
as she swaggers
into the room
to the beat
of "All About that Bass"
with a knife
the size of a machete.
She slices a cookie
into a millions pieces.
(And doesn't say a word.)
Belly Ulcer, he adds
and all of a sudden
I feel like
I've eaten

every cupcake and cookie
in the room
and now I'm gonna
throw up.
(She is still silent, slicing.)

I turn ashen
as each Oreo crumb
turns into
a spider
and crawls
off the table.
Buckle Up, Rutherford says, laughing.
(The dining room is now a hallway or an open field, I
can't tell.)

He's gone,
his laughter
now morphed into
a song
with an infectious rhythm
of blues
that's becomes the soundtrack
to a movie
with a chase scene
starring yours truly
and a big, red spider
with a dreadful face
gunning straight
for me.
(It looks familiar, but I can't tell.)

Run, she whispers
and I do
before it bites me
or worse.

I run
I run away
I run away, fast,
I run away, fast, toward—

Hovering

BLADE! BLADE! WAKE UP!
I'm awake. I'M AWAKE. What are you doing, Storm?
Stop shaking me.

Geesh, you're drenched. Wet dream, huh?
GET AWAY! What time is it?

It's half past time to get up and stop crying over spoiled milk.
Spilt milk!

Whatever, open these windows and stop whining. He messed up, get over it.
Easy for you to say, he didn't embarrass you in front of the world.

Uh, yeah he did. I was right there too. It was bad. But it's not the end of the world.
It's not the end of your world, Storm. You didn't get ruined.

He's our father, for better or for worse.
Why are you so forgiving?

Why are you not? It's a disease. He needs help.
Yeah, well, tell him that when he gets back from whatever hellhole he's in.

He's back.
Great. Now if you'll excuse me, I need some privacy.
Next time, knock.

Next time, don't scream, DON'T KILL ME, PLEASE!
What are you talking about? It was a nightmare.

What was it—fire, a cliff, a gun to the head?
It was nothing.

Still, I wanna know.
It's the same dream I've been having, Storm, but this
time, Mom was in it.

Well, now I'm intrigued, little brother.
It was ridiculous.

Get on with it, this room smells like sautéed cat pee.
. . . .

Texts from Chapel

11:45 am
*I couldn't stop
thinking about you last
night. I fell asleep*

11:46 am
*thinking about your song,
and woke up with you
on my lips. Sorry you*

11:46 am
*didn't get to
play it . . . Are you okay,
babe? Muah!*

Conversation

Yeah, and I just kept running toward her.
It's rude to text and talk.

Just gimme a sec, Storm.
It's kinda unhealthy.

What?
You're always with her, and when you're not, you're texting her. I get that you're in love and all that, but you really should get a life.

I do have a life.
What about Trenton and Roman, your best friends?

What about 'em?
You never even see them.

What are you talking about? We went to see Giraffe Tongue.
That was like a month ago.

Things change. I'm just into some different stuff.
Yeah, Chapel. It's unhealthy the way you're all up under her. Be careful, Blade.

Whatever.
What about the band? I thought y'all were gonna record.

They're more into punk now. I'm just—
Into soft rock—yeah, don't remind me.

Anyway, what do you think about the dream?
Weird dream. You been smokin'?

No. What do you think it means?
No idea.

Seriously.
Look, some dreams don't mean anything. They're just stupid.

Great, thanks, now get out.

Okay, how about this: The spider is Dad, and you think he hates you and is trying to destroy your life, and Mom is the only person who can save you, but she really can't because, you know, she's dead, and so you stuff yourself with hordes of unhealthy foods to hide the pain of whatever journey you're on.

Journey?
Yeah, "Don't Stop Believin'" journey.

That's deep, Storm. But journey where?
You tell me. It's your dream, Spider-Man.

And, what about Mom?
Well, that's easy. You miss her. We all do.

You think that's it?
Nah, you were right. It's ridiculous.

Thanks for nothing.
I changed my mind.

What?
Your room doesn't stink. You do. Take a shower.

Knock, Knock

It's been two days
since graduation.
Two days since I've
seen his face
or smelled the smell
of his rock & roll decay.

And he's knocking,
knocking the heck
out of my door
like he does
when he has a "grand"
announcement.

But what does he
have to say to me this time?
What can we possibly
say to each other?

How do you forgive
a person who ruined
what was going to be
one of the best days of
your life?

I can't imagine
what kind of peace
offering he'll bring me.

Stop knocking, I finally say.
Just come in
or go away.
He walks in
and stands at
the foot of my bed,
his arms spread out
like a fallen angel.

Conversation

Blade . . . I'm sorry, son.
. . . .

I'm leaving for a month or so.
Okay.

Don't you want to know where?
I don't.

Rehab.
Surprise.

Got my Marvels and the axe. Ready to rock!
. . . .

I think the band's really getting back together.
. . . .

Look, I'm sorry for what happened.
You think that's enough?

It's all I got.
I really don't wanna talk. Good luck.

Watch out for your sister while I'm away.
Storm can take care of herself.

She's fragile.
What does that mean?

It means her album tanked and she just needs some cheer.
Keep an eye on each other.
. . . .

I told her she could have a party. It'll help.
Great.

I need you to be there.
Dude, I got a life. You've got your rock and roll and your

drugs and alcohol, Storm's got her pretend career and—
and I'm heading to college in a few months, to get as far
away from here as possible. So, how about you guys help
yourselves.

How 'bout you stop acting like a JACK!
There's the Rutherford I know. Welcome back.

I'm still your father.
Lucky me!

*Pretty lucky, I'd say. Look around. Five-star living not
good enough for ya?*
Money doesn't buy happiness.

*Yeah, but it bought you a pimped-out Range Rover that
you and your girl make out in. And, it paid for your posh
little private high school.*
And the Harley you ruined my graduation with. Just get
out. I'm done. Good luck with rehab.

When the limo arrives

to take Dr. Feelgood
to rehab
he's all crocodile tears.
They're trying to take my edge. If I don't make it back—
Stop, Daddy, you'll be fine, Storm says.
And now she's crying.
You can do this, Daddy! We'll write kick-ass songs together
when you get back.
Rutherford looks at me. But I got nothing:
No empathy.
No sympathy
for
the devil.

Phone Conversation

Hey. Babe!
Yeah, hey.

Everything okay?
Sure.

You sure?
I've been better.

Why do you sound so salty?
Why do you think?

I'm sorry I couldn't see you after graduation. And, I'm sorry about what happened.
Just forget about it. I'm okay.

. . . .

Just wish things were different. That I was nobody in Nobody's Land.

Yeah.
So, what's up?

What's up is stay off social media and don't—
Go to stores, look at newsstands, I know.

Yeah.
I won't have to if we're together.

Awww . . . I can't right now, Blade.
Why? Come on, babe. Meet me at the park. I'll take you shopping or something in Rutherford's Maserati.

You know I'd LOVE that, but my parents are throwing me another dinner with friends tonight.
Tonight? That's nice. How come I didn't know?

I mean, it was kind of spur of the moment.
Who's invited?

Just a couple girls . . . and some people, uh, friends. Just a group of friends.

People like who? Van? Is Van going?

Blade, my parents told me to invite all my friends. You know you would be the first person on my list if my parents didn't forbid me from seeing you.

But Van, really?

My Favorite Guitarist

Sometimes
when I feel
like time is
a speedway
and my mind
races
round and round
so fast,
I walk
the dogs
to clear
my head.

Then,
I go to
Santa Monica.

Soundboard

I walk
the boardwalk
looking for Robert,
a magician
who turns worries
into songs.

In between gigs
he sits
under a
palm tree, smiling
with the few teeth
he's still got.

Tourists leave
green
in his black trumpet case,
while he
melts the *blues*,
bending the notes
like a storytelling machine,
and wailing
like the music's
gonna save him,
and us too
if we're lucky.

Conversation

Youngblood, you look like you got the blues.
Family stuff.

Yeah, how's that?
Rutherford finally did it. Lived down to his expectations.
I hate Rutherford. I loathe everything he stands for.

Whoa . . . Take a breath, Youngblood.
He's ruined everything in my life.

Everything? Sounds serious.
Graduation was a disaster to end all disasters.

How is that?
The one day I stand up to deliver a speech I wasn't
even supposed to give in front of my entire class and
everybody's grandmother, brother, and sister, Rutherford
flies in like an alien lunatic and embarrasses the life out
of me and everyone there. Even the crows were gawking
of embarrassment from the trees.

Sounds like a challenging moment.
I didn't sign up for this circus.

None of us do. It's family.
I just can't wait to get outta here.

Be careful what you ask for. You can run, but you can't hide.
You're at the crossroads, Youngblood, looking for a ride.
One of your songs?

That's life, son. Gotta be thankful for the hard and the
easy. The good and the not-so.
Hard to be thankful when you're living in hell.

Let me get this straight. You're living up in Hollywood
Hills with a pool and tennis court, and a lady to clean

*your underwear and cook you tacos on Tuesdays, and
you're living in hell. You got first world problems,
Youngblood.*

. . . .

*You can run, but you can't hide. You can run, but you can't
hide, you're at the crossroads, Youngblood, looking for a ride.*
Tell me something, Robert—why do you give all your
money away to homeless people?

So they can eat, buy a book or two.
But what about you?

What about me?
Couldn't you use the loot?

*A wise man said, "You will be enriched in every way to be
generous in every way," so I'm good.*
If you ever need a place to crash, we got plenty of space.

I try to avoid hell, Youngblood.
Look, here's a little something for you, I say, handing
him a wad of hundreds.

I don't do charity, Youngblood.
What happened to enriching and being generous?

You keep that, buy your girl some flowers or something.
You could get a new trumpet case or something, I add,
trying not to show what I'm really suggesting, but he
knows. Robert knows everything.

You still stunting on my teeth, Youngblood?
I'm just saying, it's pretty cheap these days to get 'em
fixed.

*In another life, my first wife wanted new teeth. She asked
all her friends and family for twenty-five dollars to help her
find her smile. I didn't give her a dime. The marriage didn't
last long, but good gracious did she get some pretty teeth.*

Wanna play something?

I pick up my guitar.
He picks up his trumpet.
And when the song's over,
and he's not looking,
I throw my wad of cash
in his case
and hope he's not mad
at me later.

Texts Conversation

11:14 am
Good morning, babe.
I miss you.
Guess what?

11:18 am
What's up!

11:19 am
I got my assignment. My
dorm's next to yours. WOOHOO!
Also, shopping today???

11:19 am
Hint. Hint. Wink. Wink.
You could pick me up
in your dad's Maserati.

11:19 am
He won't even know.
What time
should I be ready?

11:22 am
Oh . . .
Not sure
about today.

11:22 am
My parents are gone
all day. All night.
Their anniversary.

11:23 am
Wow. Good to hear
you have the day

open for me. Finally.

11:24 am
Blade!
Seriously?
What's up with you?

11:25 am
It's just kinda weird.
It seems all I'm good for
is buying stuff.

11:33 am
Hello, you there?

11:35 am
That was rude.
I can't believe
you'd even suggest

11:35 am
something so shallow
and beneath my
goodness. You offered before

11:36 am
so I just thought.
Never mind . . . TTYL.

11:37 am
Chapel, I'm sorry.
My bad. I'm just not
myself right now.

11:40 am
You there?
Come back.

Voice Mail

Maybe tomorrow
we can cruise
to Malibu
have a picnic
by the sea.
I'll even bring
my strings
and sing you
that graduation song.

Or we can feed
each other sorbet,
hit Rodeo Drive.
But only if
you forgive me . . .

Texts from Chapel

9:37 am
Okay. Morning!
I forgive you.
Get out of

9:37 am
your PJs pls and take
your girl for SORBETTTTTT
and Rodeo Drive!

Deliver Me

On my way
out the door
two delivery guys
show up
with a marble statue
of a naked goddess.
I cower.

I don't belong here,
and the months-long wait
'til college
is too long.
Can you deliver me
someplace else,
please . . . now? is what I want
to say
to them.

I sign
for the *Goddess Lakshmi*
while Storm
unpeels
the protective plastic
marches around
her marble legs
and marble breasts,
comparing her figure
to stone.

Her four hands represent the four goals of life, she says,
rubbing the breasts, as if they'll bring her wisdom or luck.
Oh, okay. Thanks for sharing.

Dharma and Kama, and the other two I forgot.
So, what, are you practicing Hindu now?

She's the goddess of Wealth and Prosperity. Me and Dad
ordered her for my party.

. . . .

Isn't she beautiful, Blade?

My sister is beautiful

but not in the way she thinks.
She's beautiful because
she still believes
our father's
her hero.
She trusts
in his dreams
for her.

She naively believes
she will be the next big thing
and that her position in life
is set in "stone."
This makes me feel
sorry for her
because she's clueless.

She picks up
Mick and Jagger
to celebrate the arrival
of yet another Morrison absurdity,
ceremoniously dancing
around the statue,
but the dogs get freaked out
by Lakshmi's four arms
jump out of Storm's
and smash
right into her,
sending the goddess
tumbling
off her base
and crashing
to the floor
shattering

Storm's dreams
into a million little
marble pieces.

Phone Conversation

What's taking you so long?
Had a minor emergency at our house. Leaving now,
babe.

Everything all right?
Is it ever?

We're at Rudy's

the best ice cream
in Hollywood,
and I'm telling her
how I honestly believe
my old man
could finally be changing
for the better
and that he swore
to us
he'd complete rehab—
no more drink
no more drugs—
when a white van
pulls up
and out jumps
fire-breathing paparazzi
with loaded cameras,
pushed into our faces.

How's it hanging, Blade?
Doing great. Now leave us alone.

We just got word Rutherford's back in rehab.
Yep.

*Good to know he's getting help. We want him to live. It
would be a rock-and-roll tragedy if . . .*
Really. That's enough.

We keep walking into Rudy's.
But they follow us in like
hyenas laughing,
dragons stalking.

Did you think your life was over when your old man crashed your graduation? He really knows how to liven up an event, another one chimes in.

Does it look like I think my life is over? I come at them with fists, but Chapel pulls me back.

When Doves Cry

I grip the steering wheel
like we're driving through a hurricane.

You're almost out of gas.
We'll be fine, babe.

Where are we going?
As far away from this madness as possible.

Rodeo? She puts her hand on my leg to soothe me.
Not exactly.

Finding Robert

Chapel and I walk
the pier
to find Robert,
only he's not there
or in any
of his usual spots.

I ask James, who fishes
on the pier every day, rain or shine,
to help us
find Robert.

Try Leimert Park. They got a jam session going on tonight,
he tells us.
Chapel whispers, *Another day, Blade. I should probably
get home.*

It has to be today. You have to meet him today, I say.
Seriously? Thought we were going to do Rodeo Drive.

It's important, Chapel. He's important. I need you to see.
See what?

I just need you to see . . .

We pay

the $15
to get into
5th Street Dicks Lounge
in Leimert Park,
where the musicians
jamming onstage
nearly outnumber
the people
drinking
and shimmying
in their seats.

Hearing Robert

up there
on a bona fide mic
for the first time
is like entering
a universe
where melody and
soul
and groove
and element
collide
into something strange
and magical.
She kisses me
hard and long
like a riff
strung out.

Is it possible
to overdose
on love?

He finishes his set

and waves us over.
Youngblood, how'd you find me?

I know people.
I see, he says, eyeing Chapel.

This is—
Chapel, he says, finishing my sentence.

She reaches out
to shake his hand,
but Robert doesn't shake hands.
He bows.
Chapel bows
her head too.

*It is a blessing to finally meet you, Chapel. How'd y'all like
the show?*
Pretty dope, she says.

Robert nods at Chapel. *I knew I liked you.*
It was okay, I guess.

*Okay? Boy, you better recognize . . . your little rock and
roll started in these mean streets.*
I know, I know.

*Sit down—you need a lesson, and school's about to be in
session.*

Track 3: Cross Roads Blues

ROCKER: ROBERT JOHNSON / ALBUM: *THE COMPLETE RECORDINGS* /
LABEL: VOCALION / RECORDING DATE: NOVEMBER 1936 / STUDIO:
GUNTER HOTEL IN SAN ANTONIO, TEXAS

Youngblood, don't you know
rock and roll
is just the blues
minus the hope
plus a bunch of screaming
electric guitars?

All these good ole boys
just borrowed
from gospel
and the blues.
But, don't tell them
I told you so.

Zeppelin, Clapton,
all the greats,
they just channeled
Howlin' Wolf and Chuck Berry,
and the O-riginal Robert Johnson.

Did you know
before Robert Johnson
was called
one of the fathers
of rock and roll,
he stood at the crossroads
and sold his soul to the devil
traded in his eternal residence
for guitar-playing powers
that would rock the world.

Sounds like Rutherford.

Out of Gas

That was fun.
That guy is real special. I always feel good when we hang.

We make a left on Crenshaw when my car sputters and
the engine nearly shuts off.

Blade, I told you we were almost out of gas.
It'll be fine. There's a station right over there.

Did you hear that? Is the car even on?

I tell myself everything is going to work out fine.
But I am wrong.
So wrong.

Crisis at the Pump

What are you doing here?
Mom?

WHAT ARE YOU DOING HERE, CHAPEL?

She looks at me and then at her daughter.

Blade and I went to see his friend perform at—
Chapel, you know the deal. This right here CANNOT
happen. Blade, you seem like a nice boy and I'm sure this
is hard . . .

Mom, you know how much we care about each other.
Your father and I made a decision and it's final. Now say
your goodbyes. Five minutes. I'll be in the car. Don't keep
me waiting. I would hate to tell your father.

Chapel and I embrace
frozen in fear
of this moment
we've tried to hide from.

Come on, Chapel! her mother yells from the car.
And like that
she's stripped away again.
She won't even look
out the window of the car
as they drive off.

I fill up my car
and try to fill up
the emptiness
in my spirit
on the long drive home
across a world
of canyons.

Don't fret

Mom would say
whenever I was sad.

My fingers glide
and press down
on the frets
of my guitar,
secret sounds
of pain
burning my ears,
stinging my eyes.
Hands shaking
like caffeine itself,
and it doesn't stop.
And I start thinking about
how dangerous this feels,
to love someone so much
when they can't be with you.

The Beginning of a Song

This is what I know
In this cavalcade of stars

She is Polaris
Her love shines

Brighter than one hundred suns
Sure, others are visible

But in this orbit
She is nearest

And we are bound
Together

Forever
I thought . . .

I REALLY Got to Start Locking My Door

What are you doing in here?
How about knocking?

The door was cracked.
That wasn't an invite.

More love songs for your secret lover?
Get out.

Just don't let her dad catch you.
He won't.

They all say that.
Seriously, what do you want?

Have you called Rutherford?
For what?

To see how he's doing. It's been three days.
I'm sure he's fine. Probably figured out a way to sneak in some weed.

I don't have time for this. Look, I'm having a party tomorrow night.
I heard.

Good, so you know not to be anywhere near here.
Actually, I was told to be right here.

Over my dead body.
Well, keep following in Rutherford's footsteps and you're on your way.

Jerk.
Sometimes, I think we're all cursed.

You're such a drag.
The kiss of death envelops us.

Who even says that kind of stuff?
I'm sorry.

For what?
For wallowing in the despair that is our life in front of you.

Why do you hate us so much?
I don't hate us so much.

You suck.
Rutherford's a drug addict. Our mother's dead. And we're headed nowhere fast.

Do not judge, and you will not be judged. Do not condemn, and you will not be condemned. Forgive, and you will be forgiven.

Something your shrink told ya?
You're an idiot. It's in the Bible.

Since when do you read the Bible?
We've all got stuff, Blade. Suck it up. Life's too short.

What Bible verse is that?

After she finishes

telling me
how ungrateful I am
and how *any fool*
in their righteous mind
would be more than happy
to trade places
with me
and my privileged, flashy life,
she slams
my bedroom door
loud enough
for Mick
and Jagger
to start barking.

Hope

I plop down
by the pool
stare at the ripples
and torchlight dancing
off the water.

I wonder.
About me.
I don't think I've hoped
for enough.
Maybe that's what too much money does?
Why am I so ungrateful?
I have
everything:
the cars,
the guitars,
the mansion,
the view,
the girl.

Something's not right.
There's a vacancy
inside the rooms
of my soul.
That sounds way corny,
like a bad love song,
but I've always assumed
my hope
would end
badly.
So why hope
for anything
when all the money
in the world

can't buy
a happy ending.

Hope never drowns.
That's what Mom used to say
when I was afraid to swim.
Hope swims.
I drift off, dream
of swimming
toward
a sacred shore.

Today is the Day

I wake to the feeling of
wet tongues mopping up salt
from my cheeks
and sleep from my eyes.

Instead of being ticked off
at Mick and Jagger,
I hug them, tell them
how I'm really going to miss
their insanely annoying
high-pitched yaps
and the ear-piercing songs
of their mother goddess, Storm.

But I'm going to do this.
I'm leaving LA.
I'm going to pick up Chapel
and we're going to
make a run
for the highway
and get this adventure started.

Today is the day
that hope wins.

Conversation

I tell Storm
let's Jumpin' Jack Flash
this joint—a final hurrah.

Speak English, she says.
The party. I'm gonna stay, help you out. Then, I'm ghost.

Oh lucky me!

How to Throw a Sick Party (According to Storm)

Invite every guy you've ever met
(including your exes, apparently)
and every girl you hate.

Fly DJ Goldie in
from Miami
and have her mix

your music
with music
everyone actually likes.

Have bartenders
and cocktail waitresses
pop bottles

and tubs
of shrimp
and Doritos

and hootch
(the kegs are literally labeled
hootch).

Show off
the $4000 statue
that you replaced.

Bring out
Kid Cudi, then
the dancers

you hired to perform
Bharatanatyam:
the "dance of bliss,"

which, actually, is
pretty
sick.

After the Dance

Here I stand
in a random gallery
barely noticed
by the odd-shaped faces
the loud conversations
surrounding me.
My temples pulse
like little drums
my eyes paint
scenes
each a masterpiece
of Chapel.
I wish you were here, I text
to no response,
just as Cammie Wood,
who's been sweating me
since sixth grade,
comes up
in a shoestring bikini
and smacks me
on the butt.

Conversation

Hey, sexy.
Hello, Cammie.

How's it hanging?
You tell me.

You and choir girl still together?
You mean the love of my life, Chapel?

Yadda, Yadda, Yadda!
Nice to see you.

Wait, don't go. Let's dance.
I'm good.

Your loyalty is cute. But where's hers?
What are you talking about?

She's not even here. She's probably somewhere with someone else.
Whatever. Nice chattin' with ya.

Don't be dense, Blade. Don't let church girl fool ya.
Okay, thanks, Cammie. Later.

What she won't know won't hurt her.
But it'll hurt me.

I promise to be gentle.
I have a girlfriend, Cammie. Bye!

She takes

my shades off,
gets so close
her breath tangos
with mine.

She gently kisses
my cheek,
moves around
to my ear
whispers
tasteless things
that get a rise
out of me
then she nibbles
on my earlobe.

I close my eyes.
Try not to think
about the thrill
growing.
Try to push her away
out of my mind
just before she kisses
me so hard
I'm kissing
her back.

Bliss Interrupted

Van DeWish
crashes the mic
and screams

MAY I HAVE YOUR ATTENTION!

This hater
is a wack rapper,
with rich parents
and no record deal,
who used to date
my girl,
and thus
a hater.

Ever since Storm's album
flopped,
debuting at
the last Billboard spot,
he's dissed her
on social media
every chance he gets.

But tonight is, by far, the worst.
It's live.

He gets everyone's attention,
mocking Storm's song,
then
roasts her
in front of
Her. Entire. Party.

What's the difference between you and a lawn mower? You
can tune a lawn mower. And your dad, Rutherford, is old
news.

Storm stands there
in shock,
ready to strike back. She
looks at me,
like I'm supposed
to do something.
I'm just glad Cammie's tongue
is no longer in my mouth.

Hey, Storm, Van hollers, going in for the kill, *you should
leave your band and sing solo . . . So low we don't hear
you!*

The laughter erupts
like a chorus
of mad singers,
and Storm runs . . .
she just runs,
knocking over people
and chairs
and hootch
to escape.

PARTY'S OVER

I scream
on the DJ's mic.
I don't care
where you go,
but you got
to get the heck
outta here.

We came to par-tay! Van chants, and
now everyone joins in.
WE CAME TO PARTY!

I pull the plug,
and make my way over
to him.

Get out.
It's just jokes, Blade. It's just jokes, dude.
Yeah, whatever. Party's over, everyone, I turn and say
to the posers.

I thought we was cool, Van says.
We're not.
Your girl thought I was cool, he says, laughing.

C'mon, Van, Cammie says, pulling him away before I do
something I won't regret.
It's a lame party anyway, he adds.
I clear everyone out,
make my way to the front,
where a mob
of partiers
are gawking at—

Wait, this can't—

A stretch limo pulls up

and out jumps
a scruffy
Rutherford Morrison
with two giddy girls
in matching
zebra-print miniskirts,
whose combined ages
are less than
his.

His eyes look like

they're swimming
in water.

When he comes up
for air, he waves

like everything's cool.
And a hundred

kids snap
pictures

to post
anywhere and everywhere.

After he finishes signing autographs

the limo takes
the giddy groupies away.

What are you doing here?

He holds up two fingers.
Well, son, see, that's the thing.
One: it's too cold in Denver.
Two: the rehab food was leftover prison grub. I think they
tried to poison me.
But don't worry, I have everything under control. They said
I was doing fantastic.
. . . .

Blade . . . Blade. He stumbles around,
grabs
for my shoulder
so he can balance
his wasted
soul.

Blade. Listen to me, son. I'm not gonna miss your sister's
big party. It's going to be vicious.
The party's over. You're high. This is insane.

Insane in the membrane, he says, strolling into the house
just in time for Storm
to come running
down the stairs
crying
a river
and pouring
the whole sordid mess
out for him
to drink.

Erase Me

He pushes me
up against the wall
because I didn't defend
her honor
against Van DeWish,
who he says
should have met your DeFIST!

I cleared the party.
Cleared the party? We're Morrisons, we don't clear parties.
We rock parties, and we knock the blocks off of any joker
who messes with us. What kind of weakling doesn't protect
his sister? You better wake up. The world ain't sugarcoated!
It's real out here. And if you wanna survive it, you better
learn to PULL THE TRIGGER! We don't mess around.

Yeah, and we don't quote from a comic book movie
either, is what I want to say, but he's lit, and he's not
listening to anyone but himself anyway.
Why didn't you show up?

Show up? Show Up!
You haven't shown up
in my life
since I can remember.
What do you know
about showing up?
These are things
I want to say
to him, but
all that comes out is

I'm tired of fighting.
Have you forgotten
how many times

I've defended
our name
with punches
and body slams?
He comes back with
You're not made
of rough edges
like the rest of us.
You're soft
and you've become selfish.
It's all about Blade now, isn't it?
You're wasted talent.

I peel myself
off the wall,
start to walk away,
but I just can't let this go.
You want to talk about selfish.
How about all the masses
of women you parade
around with no care
or respect.
Or your stupid addiction
to anything and everything
that kills reality.
Weak? Weak is YOU
not being strong enough
to say no.
I'm not the loser here.
As for being made like you,
you're right, I'M. NOT. LIKE. YOU!
I want nothing more
than to wipe this Morrison stench
from my body.
Clean its muddy glum

from my existence.
I'm not like
any of you.

Family Secret

You have no idea
how right you are, Storm says, getting in my face.

Storm, be quiet, Rutherford says.
No, Dad, I'm sick of his holier-than-thou-we're-all-bad-and-
he's-a-saint attitude.
He benefits from our lifestyle, and pisses on us.

Storm, I've told you, THAT'S ENOUGH!
It's not enough. Does he even know you got arrested for
almost knocking Chapel's father's lights out?

What are you talking about?
Yeah, I figured as much. You think everybody's against
you, but Dad told him that you could date whomever you
wanted and that he better not ever threaten you again.

Storm, this isn't necessary.
Yes, it is, Dad.

You're the reason Dad had to go to spend the weekend in
jail. Or what about the time you took Dad's car for a spin
and got yourself arrested 'cause you didn't have a license?
Who do you think got you off?
Well, thank you for doing what fathers are supposed to
do.

You ungrateful little—
You're right, you aren't like any of us, Storm yells.

AGREED!
You ever wonder why
you're a shade darker
than everybody in this family?
Why your hair is curly and ours isn't.
Why you play that soft stuff,

and we're Hard Rockers?

STORM! Rutherford screams. *Don't listen to her, Blade. You don't want to be a Morrison, little brother? Well, here's the kicker, you're not. You never were one of us, and you never will be . . . You're adopted!*

White Noise

I storm
out the door
buried
in silence
as if music itself
has died.

Be careful
what you ask for.

I get in the car and drive

like a mannequin
vacant and numb
to the bone.

I call her number
five times. And again.
No answer. Just her voice
saying, *You've reached Chapel.*
Sorry I missed you.
Leave me a confession.

I drive a little too fast
down Topanga Canyon
wishing my car
could turn
into a boat
and float
across the Pacific.

My phone lights up

dozens of times.
Missed calls from
Storm
Rutherford
Storm
Rutherford
Storm
Rutherford
Storm
Storm
Storm . . .

nothing from Chapel.

Text from Chapel

10:52 pm
Sorry, Blade. I've been at church all night for revival. What's up?

Texts from Storm

11:01 pm

*I know you're pissed. I
shouldn't have kirked off like that.
You're STILL my brother.*

11:35 pm

*I'm sorry. Please answer
your phone. Or call us back. Dad's
really worried, Blade.*

12:16 am

*Blade, it's been 2 hours.
Where r u? Please don't
do something stupid.*

Text from Rutherford

12:22 am

*We may not be blood, but we
are family. Sister Sledge
'til the end. Come home!*

Texts from Chapel

1:00 am
Blade, call me
so we can talk
about what happened.

1:00 am
Storm called me,
told me everything.
And that you

1:01 am
freaked out a little.
I would
too.

1:01 am
Come on, babe.
We need to talk.
You shouldn't be alone.

1:01 am
I'm getting sad
and could use
one of your hugs

1:01 am
an arm scratch
and a back rub.
A sweet song?

Under the Cherry Moon

Too shaken up
to drive,
I call a taxi,
which drops me off
a block from
her house,
in front of
blind, old Mrs. Burns,
who hasn't been seen
since 1997.

I ninja walk
down Chapel's street
where everyone is asleep
where every light is out
except for the one
in her bedroom
flickering
like a lightning bug.

Her shadow floats
across the room,
a signal
that she's still awake
and can save
my life.

Text to Chapel

1:17 am
I'm out front.
Basement window in three minutes.
Make sure they're asleep.

When the Levee Breaks

When I get
to the backyard
she's already outside

waiting to hug me
like she's never
letting go.

She cradles
my face
in her chest.

And for the first time
since the bomb dropped
I can't keep it together.

A geyser
of tears
explodes

and the weight
of my sad, sad world
bursts forth,

floods my vision.

Conversation

They didn't love me.
They gave me away
like a donation
to Goodwill.

Don't say that.

I never felt like a Morrison.
Now I know why.
Stop it. You are loved, Blade.

Am I?

Before

The sky beams
as I search
for comfort.

She wraps
her arms around
my waist.

We hug so tight,
the Milky Way spins
on *our* axis.

Our kiss
could save
a planet.

This is where I want to be.
This is where I need to be.

Swaying softly
together
toward the stars.

Until . . .

An earthquake

thunders toward us
with an anger
so fierce
it'd make ten thousand
horses fall
and never get up.

Chapel's father is
a 6.5 on the Richter.
He stomps up to me
in an ominous black robe
and practically moves
the ground beneath
us.

THIS. IS. IT. he roars.
And he tears us
completely
apart.

Aftershock

The one time
I did go to church
I don't remember
the preacher
dropping bombs
like Chapel's pastor father does
when he tells me to
GET THE—

Taking a Stand

Sir, I have been underwater
my entire life.

Your daughter pulls me up,
gives me new breath,

strange and familiar
this is all I know now.

This is where I want to be,
between the moon

and her gaze,
inside her arms

carefully inhaling
tomorrow,

is what I want to say.
What I actually say is:

SIR, I LOVE YOUR DAUGHTER!

Devastation

Chapel doesn't say, *I love him too,*
but I know she feels it,
as she squeezes
my hand so tight
the blood
hurries.

And the volcano
in his eyes
is ready to erupt.
If her mom
wasn't holding
his arm,
he'd quickly abandon
his religion.

You can try to break us up, but
you can't break our bond.
You can try to keep us apart now,
but when we go to college next month,
we'll be together, I say, standing up
like I should have done
to Van DeWish.

That so? he answers. *You love her? I bet you're a drunk like*
your father.
I get in his face.

What, are you going to hit me, like your father did? Like
thug, like son. We will see how strong your bond is three
thousand miles apart.
What are you talking about? Chapel screams.

This won't continue on my dime. You're going to
community college. Right here in LA.

Mom, that's not fair.

*Life's not fair, young lady. Get used to it. And, son, if I
were you I'd get off my property before I call the police.
NOW, he screams, like I'm a*
common criminal
whose only crime is
being in love
and alone.

Shelter

I sit under an
enormous palm tree,
a block away
from Chapel's house
in the pitch dark,
wishing I had
my guitar
to write
a song
about the second-worst
day of my life
about the shattered glass
that is my life
about the tiny shards
cutting into
Blade.

The City of Palms

I have taken for granted
the palm trees in Cali

brought in
from somewhere else

planted by Spanish missionaries
in the 18th century.

We have something
in common.

They don't belong here.
And neither do I.

Yet they stand.
How will I?

On the taxi ride home

I think
about the things
I should have said
to him
and wonder
if I'll ever
see her
again.

Maybe I've been crying
too much
or thinking
too much about
drinking this bottle
of Malibu
I took from
Rutherford,
but I don't want to
end up
like him,
especially since
I'm not
his.

When we get
to the bridge,
for a split second
I imagine
leaping over
and falling to
the bottom
and never being found
or heard from
or seen again.

Would it matter
if I were gone?
Who would care
about this son of
no one?

Change of plans, I say to the driver. Take me to Santa
Monica, please.

Perspective

I watch Robert
hold a small
audience captive
with "Mean Old World,"
which ain't nothing
but the truth
for me
right now.
I nod at him.
He smiles, and
after he's done playing,
waves me over.

Where's your other half? he asks.
I'm overwhelmed, Robert.
With gloom. She's gone, like
ashes over bridge.

He wipes down
his trumpet
and shakes
his head.

You weren't ready for her or she wasn't ready for you?
Her father wasn't ready for us. He ended it.

Put yourself in his shoes, what would you have done?
I'd trust my kid to know what was good for her. It sucks.

Sorry, Youngblood.
There's something else.

I know. Written all over your face.
I don't even know how to say it.

Spoonful at a time.
Turns out, I'm adopted.

It's like a freight train runnin' up all through your life.
It sucks.

That's one way of looking at it.
THAT'S THE ONLY WAY.

Some people don't even get one parent, you got four.
Yeah, but two of 'em gave me away, one of 'em doesn't
care about me, and one of 'em's dead.

*If the blues was cash, you'd be the richest Youngblood in
town*, he says, laughing.
Not the time for jokes, Robert. This isn't funny.

I climbed Mt. Kilimanjaro once, he answers.
Huh?

Yep, with a friend. It took seven days.
Okay! Thanks for sharing.

*Life is a mountain, Youngblood. Nobody said the climb
was gonna be easy.*
You gotta choose your route.
Get your gear.
Breathe.
Clear your mind.
And enjoy the journey.
Robert, what are you talking about?

*Perhaps you need a break from the Angels. Get outta LA,
get some perspective. You understand?*
. . . .

Give her father some time, he might come around.
You think so?

The Creator has a master plan. Y'all were meant to be, you'll be. Can't nobody stop that.
. . . .

That's a whopper of some news about your birth parents. I feel for ya. I do know this, though. There's a lot of love around you, but if you don't see it, it's not there. Go climb your mountain, see things from the top. Find out the answers you need, seek what's really important. Chapel. She's what's important.

If she's meant to shine in your life, so be it, he says, hugging me, then handing me a guitar from out of nowhere, like we're saying goodbye, and he's been expecting this all along.

Let's play one for the road, Youngblood.

I've known the rules

since I could smell
the vodka
on his breath
drown in its rancor.
I know, when it hits the fan, to:

Avoid all stores
with newsstands.
Don't watch any
entertainment shows,
and stay away
from social media
because
your family
is a trending topic
and the world laughs.

So I drive

the Sunset Strip
in search of a guitar shop
to buy a new strap
and try to clear my head.
But there with a camera
pointed like a gun
to my face
is a paparazzo
shouting,
How does it feel
to know
you're not the heir
to rock and roll royalty?

It feels

like countless mirrors
crashing around me
in an empty space
where there's
no way in
and no way out.

Day 1

I will never leave
this bedroom again.

I stare at the walls.
The ugly, empty space
imprisons me.

There is nothing
left for me
if she's gone.

A bare, unspoken
language that has
no words, no gestures—

a song
of sinking silence.

I've texted her
thirteen times.

All the Songs That Make Me Think of You

For What It's Worth
Gold Dust Woman
You Shook Me All Night Long
Tangled Up in Blue
Dreams I'll Never See
The Story in Your Eyes
Oh! Darling
Wish You Were Here
Where the Streets Have No Name
The Sky Is Falling
While My Guitar Gently Weeps
Who'll Stop the Rain?

Day 2

What is this blood
coursing through my veins?

It's not Morrison.
It's a red river
of who the hell am I.

Yesterday I was the son
of a narcissist,
but at least I knew . . .

Today it could be anyone
of the seven-plus billion
freaks and strangers
who could give
two craps about me.

Why am I even here?

Eat your food.
Freakin' A, Storm! COULD YOU PLEASE LEAVE ME
ALONE!

You must eat, she says, from the other side of the door.
. . . .

*Your life may seem like a mystery right now, but you're still
here.*
MYSTERY? TRY MISERY. I'M NOT FEEDING
THAT MONSTER.

Day 3

I open the door.
Grab the tray
of bread and pasta
pushed against the wall.
The smell of goodness
offends me.
Probably takeout,
'cause Storm can't cook.

I remember Mom
taking me to
our favorite diner
in Thousand Oaks
for their homemade rolls and honey.
She called me her sweet boy,
her precious one.

If she were here . . .
I could ask her why
she used to say,
*You can't live on bread
and love alone.*

But the real question is
how can I possibly live without *her*?
How can any of us?

Dream Variation: Soul on Fire

The dining room
is a field
of fire
and I dash
and thrash
my way
through the flames
with a big, red spider
with a dreadful face
on my heels.
(It looks familiar, but I can't tell.)
Run, Mom whispers.
So I do
I run
I run away
I run away, fast,
I run away, fast, toward
I run away, fast, toward the end.
There's an end.
And there's my mother.
And If I can get to her
everything will make sense.
I can breathe.
I'll be saved.
But I never get to her,
and right before
my soul catches
on fire
I wake up.

Funny

how your questions
never get answered
in dreams
like you're a ghost
floating
and trapped
in your own mind.

Day 4

Who are they?
Why didn't I matter enough
or at all?

How do you give up
on your own
flesh,

your own blood,
the bones you made?
How?

Storm knocks

like she's pounding a drum.
You alive? Unlock the door.

I walk over to my dresser.

Blade? I'll start singing if you don't open up.

I put on my headphones, stare
at the painting
of Mom
that I painted
when I was just three
and believed
she was my world.

I take it down
and throw it in the closet.

I grab the torn teddy bear that's wearing
a *Detroit Rocks* T-shirt
that Rutherford gave me
after one of his sold-out concerts
and toss it in the trash.

These things that
felt like security
a long time ago
were a lie.

A big lie.

The sadness

is even in the rain;
it hits the window

like a sledgehammer,
the hurt
banging away

at my nothingness.
So I do the only
thing that soothes

the only thing that fills
the void.
I write.

I Miss You

Rain rolls down my window
Reminding me of you
Feel so uneasy
'Cause I'm still crying here for you

Tell me again, why did you leave?
Don't you know without you, I cannot breathe?
I give everything, everything to feel your touch
You'll never know how much

I miss you
Don't wanna say it
Just wanna play it
'Cause I miss you!

I wish it weren't but it's true
I miss you
You had my heart, you had my soul
You had the love my heart could hold
And you simply walked away
You just walked away

I miss you
Don't wanna say it
Just wanna play it
'Cause I miss you!

I'm such a fool
And, I miss you

Day 5

A piece of paper clipped
to an envelope
slides beneath my door.

To Blade:
This is what I have.
I'm still sorry.
—Rutherford

I stare at the envelope
and chills
like an army
of fear
march up
the left side
and down
the right.

There's no one
to hold
my hand.
No one
to encourage me
to stop me
from leaving
the stage.
No drum roll.
No lead guitar
firing up the crowd.
Simply—

A manila envelope

with a Post-It note
affixed
that reads:
Lucy Pearl November, Hammond, Louisiana.
And inside
another envelope,
sealed,
with a note
on the front:

To Blade, our son,
in the event
you should want
to know more.

Love,
Mom

Day 6

I have the name
of the woman
who gave me life
and then took it away.

But

I can't see
unsealing
envelope #2
right now,
if ever.

I'm going to
shower off this pain
eat real food
empty out this sorrow
on my guitar
take this name
on the front
of this envelope
and climb.

I search

her name
and find pictures

of a young Lucy November
teaching in a preschool

in Louisiana,

but also an older Lucy November
building a school

in Ghana.

Phone Conversation

Good morning. Ark Day School.

(My heart pounds. Come on, Blade . . . speak. Just get it out.)

Hi, I'm looking for a teacher by the name of Lucy
November. I believe she's in the pre—
Lucy November?

(My head is spinning.)

Yeah. Yes. Sorry, is this the wrong school?
*Honey, it's the right school, just the wrong decade. Lucy
Pearl hasn't worked here in a long time. Can I help you
with something?*

(My breath slowly gets lost.)

No, I just needed to speak to Lucy. It's important.
*Well, I'm sorry, sweetie. As I said, she's not here anymore.
But I can put you in touch with her mother.*

Her mother? Grandmother.
No, her mother, baby.

Right. No, I know. I'm just, ugh—

(Everything pounds. Everything's real. Too real.)

You okay, sir?
I'm okay.

*Her mother is Minnie. She's in the phone book. Willie and
Minnie November.*
Thank you, ma'am.

The Call

I push the numbers
like I'm entering a code
that's going to unlock
a firewall
and every detail
and secret
will rush out
and burn me.

Each time I go
to hit the last number
I push the red button
to end the call
to stop the knowing
right in its tracks.

I can't seem to
make myself
get to the point
where there's
no turning back.

I do this
for an hour
before I call.

Conversation

Hel-lo.
Hi.

Hi. Who is this?
Ma'am, my name is Blade—

I don't need nothing else around here, young man. No more thingamajigs and whatchamacallits, so save your breath.
No, ma'am, I'm not selling anything.

If you're calling about Willie's boat, he's sold it already. For sale sign been in the yard for months, and you just calling.
I don't want a boat either, ma'am. I'm just looking for someone.

Are you the police?
I'm a, I'm a, uh, former student of Lucy November, and I just wanted to get in touch with her.

Lucy Pearl was your teacher at the Ark Day School?
Yes, ma'am.

She was a good teacher.
Yes, ma'am.

. . . .

. . . .

. . . .

Is there a chance I could speak to her, ma'am?

I reckon there is, if you were in Africa.
I don't understand.

Lucy's been in Africa for over ten years. Girl said she wanted to change the world. Determined, she was. Always talking about hope and love and Oprah.

Is she in Ghana?

Is that where they make the chocolate? At Christmas, she brings me the best chocolate I've ever tasted. I can't eat but a piece a week, 'cause it's just too sweet, you understand.
Yes, ma'am.

You're a polite young man. I guess she did a good job with you, 'cause you turned out nice.
So, is there an address or phone number?

They don't have street addresses in Ghana, she tells me. So, no mail can get to her. Plus, she's in the country part, not the city part.
Oh.

I do think I have the number to the organization she's with. They'll know where she is. Don't you young folks . . . Doogle this stuff?
Google. Yes, thank you, ma'am.

You know, you sound familiar. Have we ever met?
I don't know. It's possible.

Well, you keep doing good for yourself, young man, and if you ever get in touch with Lucy, tell her to bring extra chocolate next time. My church group always likes to meet here, and they eat up everything sweet.
I will do. Thank you for your time.

Track 4: I Was Young
When I Left Home

ROCKER: BOB DYLAN: VOCALS, ACOUSTIC GUITAR / ALBUM:
THE BOOTLEG SERIES VOLUME 7: NO DIRECTION HOME / LABEL:
COLUMBIA RECORDS / RECORDING DATE: DECEMBER 22, 1961 /
STUDIO: THE MINNEAPOLIS APARTMENT OF HIS FRIEND, *TWILIGHT
ZONE* ACTRESS BONNIE BEECHER

A sad, sad song
that Dylan
wrote
on a train
about a son
leaving
his family
in search
of closure
and salvation
that he never
finds.

Hmmm.

Day 7

I finally brush
my teeth,
wondering what life
will look like
one week,
six months,
or even a year
from now.

It's time
to find my mother,
to start
at the beginning.

I've decided
to climb the mountain
and I'm not sure what
route I'll take
or how
I'll get to the top.
But I'll start
in Ghana.

Texts to Chapel

7:39 pm
Chapel, I miss you
so much
the pain feels

7:39 pm
like a million
heart attacks.
It's time for us

7:39 pm
to jet. Together.
The world is waiting.
Let's run. Far. Fast.

7:40 pm
I'll be at the park.
Tomorrow, 7:30 pm.
Meet me, babe.

Conversation

AFRICA?!
Yup.

Long way to go to, little brother, to find some woman who threw you away.
It's what I have to do.

Halfway around the world, and you're not even sure if she's there.
She's with an organization that does work in Ghana. I found all the info online.

Yeah, trust the Internets, why don't you?
Hey, if she's not there, I'll just go on safari.

Safari's in East Africa, Blade.
Oh, well, it'll be a vacation before I go off to college.

I'm worried about you, Blade.
Really? Well, if you're so "worried" about me, then why didn't you tell me sooner that I was adopted? How come you knew before me? That's just not cool.

Ugh. I feel terrible. I overheard Dad and Uncle Stevie talking one night, a coupla years ago, about a special letter Mom had written for you. I asked him why she hadn't written one for me. I wanted to tell you, swear, but he made me promise to keep it a secret, that he was saving the letter for . . .
Whatever. Save your breath. I don't want you to cry.

Everyone's been worried.
Too late for that.

We love you, you know?
. . . .

Isn't it cliché to go looking for your birth parents?
That's real sensitive, Storm.

I'm serious. She gave you up. Let her be.
I can't.

You should talk to Dad first.
I don't have anything else to say to him.

That sounds about right. I'm sure Mom would co-sign that attitude if she were alive.
She would. She's been trying to tell me something in my dreams for a while now.

Look, Blade, right now you have a father who, despite the fact you think is a super freak, loves you, and you have an amazing, talented sister . . . the best in the world, really. You give up on us, you got nothing.
Maybe.

Go talk to him, Blade.
Where is he?

Follow the music.

Down the hall

past the library
of sheet music
and comic books,
into the foyer
of statues
and ghosts,
the strum of
memories melts
into the air
like a mirage
of a life
that was once there.

The chords are
unmistakable.
They belong
to my mom
and to him.
I follow the sound
out to the pool.

He is rocking
back and forth
weaving a song
with his fingers.
The pain in those strings.
The look on his face
says love never dies off
never leaves
the secret chords
of the heart.

Track 5: Sunny

ROCKER: BOBBY HEBB / ALBUM: *SUNNY* / LABEL: *PHILLIPS* /
RECORDING DATE: 1966 / STUDIO: BELL SOUND STUDIOS, NEW
YORK CITY

This is the song
Rutherford played
between tears
at her funeral.

It's the only
non-rock song
I've ever heard
him sing.

It's been covered
hundreds of times
by everyone from Cher,
to Leonard Nimoy (Yep,
Dr. Spock from *Star Trek*),
to Bryan Adams,
to James Brown,
to that kid, Marvin Gaye Washington,
on Showtime's *Ray Donovan*.

When Rutherford sings
"Sunny,"
it's like an eruption
of joy and pain.
To hear him
croon
is to know
his hurt
is volcanic
is to know
he is capable

of loving
even if he refuses
to ever show it.

Bobby Hebb
wrote it
forty-eight hours after
two tragedies:
The assassination
of President Kennedy
and the murder
of his older brother,
Harold, who
was stabbed
outside a
Nashville nightclub.

Rutherford would never
record it
for an album,
but he loves it
like it's his,
probably because
he can relate
to the stinging sorrow.

But mainly,
he loves it
because of
the title.

It's Not Enough

He finishes.
Bowed head,
lowered eyes.

I'm leaving.
I found her.
I fly tomorrow, I say.

He looks at me,
defeated,
says nothing, but

Sorry.
Yeah, me too.

Conversation

You're really doing this.
Bought my ticket, so yeah.

You're just gonna pack up and go to Africa.
Yup.

What about shots and pills? You could get malaria or
something.
I got it covered, Storm.

She walks over,
gives me a punch in the arm,
then a hug.

I never told you this because
I thought it would go to your head.
A lot of girls liked you. I mean A LOT.
I was always afraid you would change,
become arrogant and pompous.

Like you?
Shut up. I told them all your weird habits.

What weird habits? I don't have habits.

We look at each other.
Really look at each other.
Two siblings connected
through experiences
that forever changed us
and now separated
by our blood
and the truth.

Will you call me? Text me?
I'll think about it.

You suck.
Can you do me a favor?

What?
Before I leave
I want to give Chapel a gift
to let her know
she'll always be
with me, on my mind,
and deep inside
my skin.

That's real romantic. Ugh!
Can you call her house for me? She's not answering her
cell.
Remind her to meet me
at the park
tonight, 7:30.

Sure.
Uh, like now, please.

Sure, soon as I finish reading the Report. *We're famous
again.*

. . . .

Hollywood Report

Breaking News: After initial reports, it has now been confirmed
that Rutherford, and his late wife, Sunny, Morrison's son, Blade,

is not their biological child.
He was adopted as a newborn.

According to sources, his birth mother, Linda December,
lives in Mississippi or Louisiana, and

gave him up to pursue a singing career.
How the Morrisons kept this family secret

out of the press for almost eighteen years
is nothing short of miraculous.

Blade Morrison, spotted at the home of his ex-girlfriend,
is now MIA.
It's safe to say that we can all expect the unexpected

when it comes to the Morrisons.

I pack up what matters

A bottle of malaria pills
Passport
iPad with 4245 pictures of us,
most celebrating
her blue eyes,
Guitar and guitar pics
Graduation gift wallet
Copy of *Charlotte's Web* (the one Mom read to me five
times)
Storm's terrrrrible record
Clothes that smell like here
A pillow with a thousand tears
The teddy bear Rutherford gave me
The unopened letter from Mom
Sliver of faith.

And, then I go
to honor
Chapel.

Conversation

Where do you want it?
Right here, on my bicep.
To honor my girl
and her patience,
'cause I'm about to leave town
and I don't know
how long I'll be gone.

You look familiar.
I'm just a small-town boy.

*Show me a picture of what you want done and let's get
started.*
I just want her name in a cool font. And maybe a flower.
How long will it take?

However long the muse takes. First tat, huh?
Yeah.

Buckle up, kid, it may sting a bit.

A Bit?

The pain
is almost instant.
He begins his work
and it feels like
someone's nails
scratching the heck
out of a bad sunburn.
And I'm just
begging that
the muse moves
a little faster.

It Feels Permanent

What if Chapel thinks
I'm crazy
for declaring
my undying love
this way?

What if she thinks I'm
a pathetic freak
and runs
in the other direction?

I remind myself
how much we've been through
and how we could move
canyons and seas
stars and planets
together.

But what if she thinks I'm crazy?

I decide to drive to Robert
to see what he thinks,
and to say goodbye.

Gone, Like He Was
Never Really Here

Goodbye man,
is what
I want to say.

I love you, man
is another.

I hope
we see each other again
someday.

But none of these things
are given voice
because,
according to Jimmy,
Robert left Cali
on a tour
three days ago,
replanted himself
like a palm
in another
distant land.

Leaving Chapel

I pull into the park
and turn off the car

sit with my windows down
listening to the teasing sound

of couples laughing,
planning their futures.

It's the loneliest, cruelest sound
in the world.

How do I tell Chapel
I'm leaving?

Maybe she will come.
Maybe she will break out

of her parents' prison?

Text Conversation

8:33 pm
Storm, where's Chapel?
Did you text her?
I'm gonna head over.

8:33 pm
Yes. Come home first.
I need to talk with you.

8:34 pm
Why?
What's up?

8:35 pm
Blade, come home, please.

I imagine

she jumps into my arms.
We kiss.
Our lips
like two special edition
book covers
keeping our
secret story
safe inside
the history book of
greatest loves.
I tell her I'm leaving,
she insists
she's going with me.
And that we're never
coming back.
We'll compose
some deep cuts—
flip the script—
our B-side
in a place
that's just ours.

I see

the lights
still on
in Chapel's bedroom window.

Why am I so nervous?
Her parents are at church. I know this because I called
the church.
So who is that laughing around back?

I slowly
make my way
around to the giggling
and see
her silhouette
in the dusk.
My girl
with—

Van DeWish

Tickling each other
in *our* hammock.
Locking lips.

This. Can't.
Possibly. Be.
Happening.

They hear the fallen branch
snap under my feet
and look straight at me.

The cruel moon
decides to
make an appearance

right now,
right over the place
where we've made out.

Eight Legs and Fangs

Blade, what are you doing here?

Van falls out of the hammock, like I've done
a million times before.

There are no words.
There is no breathing.
I wonder if my heart
is even still beating.

Oh man, dude. Sorry, it's just not your year.
We had a thing first. Remember?

I rush him.
Ready to finally knock
his block off
like I shoulda done
at the party.

Chill, man.
Chapel steps in front of me,
sees my new tattoo.
A tear falls
from her face.

Dang, dude, that's a dope tattoo, Van says.
I could die right here. Am I still alive?
I'm so sorry. I wanted to tell you in person, Blade, but not
this way. I know you're upset.

He didn't look upset when Cammie Wood had her tongue
down his throat.

I look her in those blue eyes.
The deep blue sea.
I'm drowning.
Blade, say something, please, she says.
So I do.

You're the spider.

Crying

Ever heard
the sound
of goodbye?
The way a door closes.
The way a deer looks.
The way a busted bird sings.
The ending of the world.
The wailing of
a hollowed heart.

You're Excused

Saturday, late night
Holding him tight

Sunday, upset
Instant regret

I'm not gonna cry no more
I'm just gonna laugh at all your tears

I don't have to try no more
Might as well just write off all these years

And while I'm at it
Can't forget it
I got one more question, Boo
Is it that easy . . . to get with you?

Princess weaving
Hero heaving

Wicked Chapel
Poisoned apple

I'm not gonna cry no more
I'm just gonna laugh at all your tears

I don't have to try no more
Might as well just write off all these years

And while I'm at it
Can't forget it
I got one more question, Boo
Is it that easy to get with you?

Monday, I said you looked fine and I lied
Your hair was frizzy

Tuesday, your breath smelled so bad that I cried
My eyes grew dizzy

Wednesday, I wondered if you were still mine
Man, I was crazy

Thursday, I bought you those jeans so Divine
And, girl, you played me

I'm not gonna cry no more
I'm just gonna laugh at all your tears
I don't have to try no more
Might as well just write off all these years

And while I'm at it
Can't forget it
I got one more thing to say

You're the freakin' spider.

© BLADE MORRISON

196

The heart

is a small
and lonesome place
she is a country

her eyes hold
the river
I used to swim

her skin,
the morning fruit
I touched and tasted

the heart is a small
and lonesome place
she is a country

I no longer live in.

I decide

I will not let
her betrayal
or theirs
ruin one more day
of my screwed-up life.

If Rutherford and Sunny
hadn't been musicians,
they would have never met,
or adopted me
into this circus.

There would have been
no encores.

If I hadn't gotten drunk
on love songs,
I would have never fallen
for her.
I'd still be singing,
not bruised, tattooed, and tattered.

I take the cause
of all this pain,
lift it
over my head,
and SLAM.

SLAM it
to the ground
until it hurts.
Until it can't hurt anymore.

I raise a hammer,
SMASH up
what's left

rip out
all the strings,
DESTROY
all the love
that was
once played.

I am done
with music,
rock & roll,
and LA.

The End.

Shattered

You can't destroy that guitar!
Watch me.

*Blade, that's that one Dad gave you. That's a Van Halen
Frankenstrat. WHAT ARE YOU DOING?*
I don't care what it is, or who made it. It's an anchor
weighing down my life. It's a curse.

She looks at the rage in my eyes and then she sees . . . my
arm.

Oh no. What did you do?
Did you know? TELL ME!

. . . .
Why didn't you tell me?

I tried to get you to come home so I could—
I'm outta here. This place is rotten, and I can't be in this
stench one more second.

You're not right. You shouldn't go.
If I stay here, I'll never be right.

Don't do this, Blade!
I'll see you, sis.

Can I take you to the airport?
No.

Wrong answer. Plus, I got your keys.

Storm and I stare

at the mangled masterpiece
scattered across
my room.

I can't believe
I destroyed
an Eddie Van Halen *Frankenstrat.*

Who does that?

I feel like Frankenstein
has taken my monster
of a life,

ripped out
all the empty parts:
brain, spine, ticker.

What's left?

And now
it's up to me
to put myself back together,

to rebuild.
To start from zero.
Storm grabs my hand.

I guess it had to happen, Blade. C'mon. Let's go.

Leaving LA

I won't miss
the Hollywood Hills,
the palm trees,
the fake city
and its manufactured lights.

I won't miss the blood suckers,
those paparazzi,
and the tabloid news,
shame because of my name,
or even
those sunsets over
Santa Monica Pier.

I won't miss this pain
that will never leave.
I won't miss
the music under the trees
or the feeling
of finding my own
safe place to breathe.

And now, I won't miss her.

Before Takeoff

You want me to park and walk you in?
Don't waste your time.

I can come with you.
Bad idea. Plus, don't you have another bad album to
record?

. . . .

I'm just kidding.

You're right, I'm not good. But I love it, and maybe I'll get
better.
You can have my room if you want.

I'd need to get it fumigated first.
Ha!

Seriously though, if you postpone your trip until tomorrow,
I'll go home and pack and we'll meet your birth mother
together.
I should do this on my own.

Blade Morrison, flying solo.
Yeah, something like that.

. . . .

. . . .

Okay, well, get out of my car.
Bye, Storm.

Oh, I almost forgot, a gift for you, little brother.
A mixtape?

I know you still carry that CD player Mom gave you.
Thanks. What's on it?

Best rock bands ever.
Guns N' Roses?

Yeah, you're a Morrison. We're hard. Time to nix all that Tears for Fears crap.
What are you talking about? "Everybody Wants to Rule the World" is Top Five, easily.

Top Five bubble gum rock.
Rock is rock.

Said the boy who dreams of Meghan Trainor.
My big sister is a rock bigot! I had no idea.

I love you, Blade. I wish more than anything, you find what you're looking for.
Me too.

Track 6: Welcome to the Jungle

ROCKERS: GUNS N' ROSES / ALBUM: *APPETITE FOR DESTRUCTION* /
LABEL: GEFFEN RECORDS / RECORDING DATE: JANUARY–APRIL,
1987 / STUDIOS IN LA: RUMBO STUDIOS, TAKE ONE STUDIO, THE
RECORD PLANET, CAN-AM STUDIO

They say
Axl Rose wrote
the lyrics
while visiting a friend
and thinking back
to when
he first arrived
on the LA scene.
Before his fame.
Before the temptation.
Before the pain.
A dog-eat-dog world.

I've lost too much here,
bled too much there,
among the beasts.
And I'm not gonna die
in this jungle.
You can't bring me
to my knees.
I'm leaving
all you savages
behind.

Part Two:

West Africa

Cramped

Five hours
after takeoff
I have to give up
my cushy first class seat
with steak
and gelato
to board
a connecting flight
that only had
one seat left.

In coach.

Regrets

I realize
that finding
my birth mom
was a great idea
in theory.

What will I say to her?
Who is my father?

What will she say to me?
Do you hate me?

I listen
to Storm's mixtape,
clinging to
Sunny's letter,
wishing I were
in my roomy home
in my own
comfy bed.

Track 7: Enter Sandman

ROCKERS: METALLICA / ALBUM: *METALLICA* / LABEL: ELEKTRA /
RECORDING DATE: JUNE 16, 1991 / STUDIO: ONE ON ONE STUDIOS,
LOS ANGELES

This is what happens
when you let Storm
pick your music.

I hate the song,
but it captures me
in its web,
taunts me
like a wrestler
strutting
into the arena
to fight.

Haunts me
like the men
and women
marching
cold blooded
into battle.

I can't help
but play it again,
to feel the rage.
It jabs me
to sleep
thinking of how
against the world
I feel
flying in
and out of it.

Dream Variation: The Ledge

It's still red velvet
on the table,
but this time
Chapel's here
seated in
a white tee
with **SB**
emblazoned
on it.
That's an easy one, Scarlet B—, Rutherford says, before
Mom interrupts him
with a look
that says, *Behave.*
This makes me laugh.

Mom, still slicing
the cookie
into a millions pieces,
doesn't say a word.
Sunny Bye, he adds,
blowing a kiss
to Mom
then disappearing
with a fork
that looks
like a guitar.
Chapel is crying,
or laughing,
I can't tell.

When the cookie crumbs
turn into
spiders
and crawl

off the table,
I want them each
to sting her
to make her feel
the pain
I see when
I look
at her.
So Blue.
Sorry, babe, she says,
and then she's gone.
And then it's just me
and Mom.
And the dining room
is now an open field.
And a big, red spider
with a dreadful face
is gunning
straight
for me.
Run, Mom whispers.
So I do.
I run
I run away
I run away, fast,
I run away, fast, toward
I run away, fast, toward the end.
There's an end.
Finally, there's an end
with a ledge.
And there's my mother.
And if I can get to her,
and if I can jump,
I'll be saved.
And the world

will make sense
again.

Blade, how about you play something else?
Huh?

Metallica, really. What happened to my kinder, gentler,
little rock and roller?
Wait, what are you doing here?

Sitting

next to me
thirty-thousand feet
over the Atlantic
on a ten-hour flight
to Ghana
to find
my mother
is
my mother?

Conversation?

You look confused.
What are you doing here?

I think you know the answer.
Uh, no, I don't. Is this real?

It's as real as you need it to be.
I miss you, Mom. We all miss you so much.

Things are outta control, it seems.
Way outta control.

That's why you left?
I left to find my family.

. . . .

I'm sorry, I didn't mean it like that. I just mean without knowing, I feel empty.

I can dig that.
I don't understand. How are you here?

You're asking the wrong question, Blade.
I am?

You're at the crossroads, looking for a ride. The question is, where are you going?
Ghana.

Yeah, but when you get there, where?
According to the website, a village. In the east.

And when you find what you're looking for?
I don't know, but it's gotta be better than this.

It won't get better, until you help him.
Who?

Who do you think?

I'm done with trying to help him. He's ruined my life too many times. I need to move on.

I'd ask you to play me a song, but, well, your guitar . . .
How do you know about that?

A mother knows. She always knows.
I'm still dreaming, aren't I. This isn't real.

Youngblood, this is as real as it gets. Just me and you flyin' through the sky, between the moon and the deep blue sea.
Why'd you call me Youngblood?

That's Jimi Hendrix.
I knew that. "Angel," right?

Best song ever. You know why he wrote it?
Probably about a woman.

About his mother. He had this dream, and she was on a camel, and in it she told him she wasn't gonna be seeing him too much anymore, and two years later—
She died.

You figure out who the spider is?
I can't even say her name.

Try again.
She broke my heart.

Stop running.
Huh? But, you been telling me to run.

Run toward, not away.
Away from what? I'm confused.

Wake up, Blade. Face the spider.

I wake up

as the plane lands,
and my ears pop
like knuckles.

I'm afraid
to open my eyes
and not find her here.

Welcome to Ghana, says the flight attendant.

We exit
onto the tarmac
under blinding sun

and even though
she's gone
I feel promise.

The heat

swallows
me whole

even my sweat
is sweating.

The sign
in the entrance hall says

AKWAABA.
WELCOME.

But there is nothing
welcoming

about no AC
and soldiers

with AK-47s
checking me out

as I approach customs
drenched

and a little
scared.

Outside

of the airport
in Accra,
what hits me faster
and harder
than the torrid sun
are the loud
taxi drivers
boiling
in anger
who try
to seize
my suitcase
while arguing
like boxers
in a ring.

Lucky me,
I choose the taxi driver
with no AC
who listens
to Garth Brooks.

On the way to the village, we pass

gas stations
and malls
and condos
and fancy cars
and junksters
and traffic lights
and traffic
and car horns
and road rage
and more traffic
and homeless
and women
carrying kids
on their backs
and tubs
on their heads
filled with
plantain chips,
coat hangers,
pillows, and
everything
you could possibly
ever need
to buy.

Conversation with Taxi Driver

My brother from America? he asks, in an almost-British
accent.
Yes.

Trump country.
. . . .

Is America great again, he says, more like a joke than a
question.
How far is the drive?

Can't drive too fast on these roads.
How much is the fare to Konko, sir?

Not too much.
Apparently, Ghanaians don't answer questions.

First time in Ghana?
Yes.

What's in the east?
I'm going to see family.

Right. That's a good thing.
. . . .

We have rainy season now, boss.
That'll be good, 'cause it's crazy hot.

*Sorry no AC. I can get it fixed. You need a driver while
you're here, then Mr. Easy is your guy,* he says, handling
me a card.
I think I'm good.

This is your American music. Like it?
I'm more of a rock and roll fan.

Kendrick Lamar! Yeah, I like him too.

Not exactly, but cool.

LeBron James.
What?

You know LeBron James?
Nah, you're funny. Hey, do you happen to have an
iPhone charger?

I don't, but she does, he says, pulling over to the side of
the road, almost hitting a girl with a dozen chargers
strung over her shoulder.

Like I said,
everything
you could possibly
ever need
to buy.

Texts from Storm

1:25 pm
You make it okay?
What time is it there?
Are you awake?

1:25 pm
Dad's doing better.
He woke me up EARLY
to record. Believe that!

1:25 pm
I think we got a
future hit, Blade.
Hope you like it!

1:26 pm
Lyrics are sad, but
I think it may be THE ONE.
He says it's perfect

1:26 pm
because there's real
motion in the emotion.
Chapel caught Van

1:26 pm
with Cammie. Karma
is a beast. Miss you, little
brother. How's Africa?

Texts to Storm

1:31 pm
This place is
beautiful and dirty.
Sorta like us.

1:31 pm
Kind of a mix
between New York
and Mississippi.

1:31 pm
Crowded and sparse
at the same time. Desolate,
but not neglected. Anyway,

1:32 pm
I'm headed to a village
called Konko to find
Lucy. Not sure if this

1:32 pm
is all going to work out.
Not even sure I'm
gonna make it to the

1:32 pm
village. These roads are
BADDDDDD! and the taxi
drivers are worse.

1:33 pm
HELPPPPPP!
BTW, good luck
with the song!

Junction

After two hours
of winding
cratered roads
in a beat-up Honda
with no shock
absorbers
to absorb
the shock
of forty-seven miles
of unpaved roads
with scattered potholes,
the taxi driver
finally stops.

Konko, he says, and points
to a long road
on the right
of the junction.
Thank you. Mr. Easy, I respond. How far of a walk?

Not far. Maybe four. Maybe five.
Minutes?

Kilometers.
. . . .

The Morrisons

have fast cars
and drivers
and sometimes
we don't even walk
from the main house
to the tennis court.
That's what
golf carts
are for.

But today,
beneath copper sun
I walk
past skinny pigeons
and skinnier goats
for what
seems like
weeks
down a long, hot,
red dirt road
that scalds
through my memories
and seems
to never
ever
end.

Two Hours Later

The girl
getting water
has a smile
that glows
and flows
like the waterfall
her midnight arms
pump
into pails.

Hello, I say.

Hello, she replies
not looking up,
with an accent
so thick
and smooth
it rolls
off her tongue
like butter.

Conversation

Hi, do you speak English?
Yes, boss.

I'm looking for Konko.
Well, you have found it.

Cool.
I am Joy. Welcome.

That's your name, Joy?
It is. And you are?

Blade.
Blade, like the American movie with Wesley Snipes?

That's it.
Are you a superhero?

Not at all.
Well, it is nice to meet you, Mr. Blade.

Nice to meet you, Joy. Are you from England?
Why do you say that?

Your accent, there's, like, hints of British. The taxi guy
too.
Hmmm. Colonization. Blame it on the queen.

Right.
You could use some water, it seems.

That was a very, very long walk.
Only if you've never done it.

You've done it?
Twice a week. Some of my students, twice a day.

. . . .

Down the road, over there is a shop. We can get some

bottled water there.

I don't mind drinking the well water.
Even with your American malaria pills, this water is not safe.

Well, can I help you with the water?
No, Mr. Blade, I can handle it.

Three buckets of water and two arms—are you sure?
I have been carrying buckets since I was three. I am sure.

If you say so.
So tell me, Mr. Blade, what are you doing here?

Looking for someone.
Detective Blade.

Not like that. I think my mother is here.
There are no other missionaries here but you, I'm afraid.

I'm not a missionary.
All Americans who come here are on a mission.

I am on a mission, but it's just to find my birth mother.
Interesting. You are not here to save us?

I got enough problems of my own, trust me. I'm here to close a chapter.
I see. Well, what is your mother's name?

Lucy. Lucy November.
Lucy November is your mother?

I think so. So you know her?
Yes, I do. Lucy November is my auntie.

So, we're cousins?
Not exactly.

I don't understand.

It is a sign of respect, in Ghana, for women who take
responsibility for nurturing and protecting, who look
out for the children in their lives like Ms. Lucy does. It is
protocol to say Auntie.

So, can you take me to her?
I can't, but I know who can, Blade. Come, I will explain.

Joy walks

like
she could balance Venus
on her head.
Not a drop of water
spills
from the two medium pails
on each hand
or the large bucket
centered
on her head.

How is that possible?

She doesn't trip
on a stone
or tree root,
or look to find
her steps.
She just knows
the way
of the sun
and her hips
sway like a wave
keeping time.

She stops,
turns around,
fluid
like the water,
and looks at me.

Are you staring, Mr. Blade?
I'm not staring. But you can at least let me take one.

I am fine. Medase!
That means thank you, right?

It does. And I do thank you. But, I've got this.
Akwaaba!

I am welcome?
You said, *Thank you,* I was saying, *You're welcome.*

Ahhh! Yennaase *is "you're welcome."*
Oh, sorry about that.

It's okay, Blade, you're trying. Most American's don't.
Joy, how far are we walking?

Not too far—we're close.
. . . .

Twenty minutes later

we arrive
at a house—
if you can call it that—
made out of
red dirt
and slabs of wood.

Just put your bag down over there, she says, pointing to a
pile of rocks and a pot.
So, where can I find Lucy?

*Konko is a big place. There are almost a thousand people
spread throughout it. Most are here, but there are some in
a neighboring community, and a small group in a remote
settlement. Auntie Lucy is visiting there.*
In the settlement. Why?

*They do not have a lot up there. Even less than we have. She
goes to help. With school. With medicine. With food.*
How far is it?

Not—
Yeah, not far, I know. How many miles?

Twenty-five kilometers, but you will need a guide.
A guide?

*It's on the other side of mountain and rainforest. You can
drive for a quarter of the way. The rest is walking, and you
will need a guide.*
And where might I find the guide?

He goes up once a week.
When is the next time he's leaving?

He left this morning.
Can we call her?

No Reception

Of course,
there are no
working cell phones
in that remote
settlement
because there are no
cell towers
on the other side
of mountain
and rainforest.

Perhaps we can send
an African pigeon
with a note,
I want to say
in frustration.
But, of course,
I don't.

It is impolite

to turn down
a dinner invitation, she says,
handing me a bottle
of Volvic water.

How much do I owe you?
Three cedis.

I haven't exchanged my money yet. How much is that?
Oh, sixty dollars.

Very funny.
My treat, she says,

pounding flour
and water
in a bowl
along with several
other women
in the village,
while they speak
in a language
I can't understand,
though I can tell
they are talking
about me
by the laughter
and the stares.

Her Village

is bustling
and bursting
with children
chasing goats
and soccer balls,
while their mothers
cook, wash, laugh,
and dance
all at the same time,
to what sounds like
James Brown,
only faster,
with heavy drums
and lots of chants.

The energy here
is familial,
jovial even.
It rivals Hollywood Boulevard,
only less glitz
more raw
and real.

The men are off
cutting timber
growing cocoa
farming
all day
for their families.

Each person
I pass
waves
like they know me
or they want to.

It is a good feeling
not to be recognized
and still noticed.

Track 8: Zombie

ROCKER: FELA KUTI / ALBUM: *ZOMBIE* / LABEL: COCONUT RECORDS / RECORDING DATE: 1975 / STUDIO: NIGERIA

The music they're dancing to, what is it?
Fela. FELA KUTI! Rabble-rouser.

Sounds like funk jazz rock dance music all mixed up.
The king of Afrobeat.

This song is long. It's been playing forever.
Epic songs. Some are ten, some are twenty minutes long.

He's Ghanaian?
From Nigeria, but all of Africa loves Fela.

Where is the music coming from?
There is a boom box and big speakers in a truck down the way. DJ Enoch entertains us.

A boom box? Wow! Haven't seen one of those in a while.
The song is called "Zombie." But, not your American zombies. It's about soldiers who don't think for themselves, they just follow orders. The song got him into a lot of trouble.

Like what?
Ironically, he was banned from Ghana. And because of the song, the very soldiers he spoke out against were ordered to kill his mother.

Did they?
The zombies did.

For a song? That's crazy.
Music is powerful, Blade.

Fufu

For dinner,
I hesitantly eat
what looks like
dough
and tastes
like nothing good
until
I dip it in a bowl
of peanut soup
and eat every last
piece.
And when it's gone
I try to eat
what lingers
on my fingers.

Conversation

Where will you stay tonight?
Do you have hotels?

There are plenty back in Accra. A few near the junction.
You mean back up the long hike?

*Taxis will come, but they are random in the evening. More
in the mornings.*
Seriously?

There's always tomorrow.
Medase.

I hear sarcasm.
. . . .

There is a bed in the school. You can sleep there.
What about a shower? Anywhere around here to do that?

What do you think the water was for, boss?
Of course.

On the way

to the school
something runs
in front of us,
and when I ask
Joy what it is,
she smiles, and says,
If we're lucky,
tomorrow's soup.

Conversation

That's not funny at all.
It most certainly isn't.

Where I come from, that was a rat. A big ole rat.
Grasscutter is a delicacy.

I'll pass.
So what brings you here to talk to your mom, Lucy? You know, I had no idea she had a son.

I just found out that I was adopted.
And who are your adoptive parents now?

My mother died when I was eight.
Koo se. I am sorry.

My father and sister are back home.
They must miss you, yes?

It's complicated.
Is it?

Where is your family?
They live in Volta region.

How far is that?
A long way.

So, why are you here?
I came to take care of my uncle. He is old and doesn't see.

I'm sorry.
You are sorry a lot. It's life, Mr. Blade.

Please just call me Blade.
These are your quarters, Blade.

This is your school?
This is it.

Oh.

Home

We are
in a building,
if you can call it that,
smaller than
my Hollywood bedroom.

It has three rooms
no doors
no windows.
We stand in the largest.

I can see
the stars
through holes
in the roof
held up
by four logs
shooting up
from a dirt floor
with rows
and rows
of chairs
and a cross,
which lets me know
this is also a church.

God help me.

Conversation

We will make a pallet over there, she says, pointing to a
wooden contraption with a few blankets on top.
Wait, is this a church? I thought you said I'd be sleeping
in the school.

*This building is, indeed, the church, Blade. And the
community center. And the library. And the school. It's not
complete, but we are working on it.*
I see. Don't get me wrong, I appreciate it, but I'm happy
to pay for a bed, in a house or something.

*All the extra space we have is occupied by children who
have lost their parents.*
Lost their parents?

*Yes, many have left to find work, or have fallen sick.
Millions here are affected by malaria. Parents die or are
too sick to take care of their sick children. We have twenty
thousand children die each year from it. The mosquitoes
are treacherous.*

. . . .

*Don't worry, Blade, we have mosquito nets. Plus, your
American pills are potent.*
I'm sorry, Joy.

Don't be. It is not your fault . . .
What happens to the orphans?

Orphans

The word seems sad
when you say it.

An orphan
is like a soul bulb

waiting
to be planted

in just
the right place.

When you're an orphan,
you no longer belong,

but a child is a child
of everyone,

they belong
to a community,

to a greater garden,
she says.

But what if the garden is barren? I think,
still captivated
by the way she talks
by the way she cares
by the way
the moon
paints
her perfect
face.

I see you are staring again.

Portrait of a Woman

I am no Michelangelo
I prefer music
to mezza fresco

this old tree
is my canvas
and I marvel

at your body
and soul
the masterpiece

that is your
pristine walk
the heavenly way

it colors
the world
from earth

to sky.
I want to write
your song,

is what I want to say, but
what comes out is:
Can I get that mosquito net, please?

Conversation

You should rest, my friend. The roosters will be here soon.
And with them come eager children who want to meet the
American boy.
I doubt if I will sleep with the big rats looming.

Oh, they are more afraid of you than you are of them.
You sure about that?

Positively. What you must keep your eye out for are the
mountain lions, she says, laughing so loud even the
crickets stop to listen.

Her smile
makes me forget
that I am
seven thousand miles
away from
the spider
that bit
and poisoned me.

I dig through my suitcase

for my malaria pills
beneath the iPad
with 4245 pictures of Chapel
I can no longer look at,
guitar picks I no longer have use for,
wallet with too much money
yet never enough
to help me make sense of this life,
Charlotte's Web,
which makes me think too much
of the spider in my dreams,
the clothes and pillow
that smell like home,
until I reach
Mom's sealed letter
that taunts me
that scares me
that I hold
while I drift off
to the unfamiliar hum
and frantic patter
of a Ghanaian night.

Text Conversation with Storm

4:45 am
I think I only slept
for four hours.
Jet-lagged like crazy.

4:45 am
Plus the roosters started
crowing like thirty minutes ago.
You finish the song?

4:45 am
Stop blowing up my
phone, Blade. I'm busy.
Studying ciphers.

4:45 am
Ciphers? What are you,
a rapper now?

4:46 am
Kabbalah. Don't hate.
Madonna does it too,
I think.

4:46 am
Whatever works. Express
Yourself! LOL!

4:47 am
Storm, you still there?
I slept in a makeshift
school last night.

4:47 am
It's really just dirt
and concrete. Next stop,

hotel.

4:47 am
*BLADE, what part of stop
bothering me did
you not get!!!*

4:47 am
The whole place is a
work-in-progress, actually.

4:47 am
Boy, bye.

zZZZZ

An hour later, when the
roosters take a break, I fall
back asleep and dream

of nothing.

This Morning

Last night,
after missing
the gentle strum
of my guitar
that always helps
me find
my slumber
and finally
passing out
from the boiling heat,
and then
waking up
at three am
and thinking
of all the things
I'm going to say
to my mother
and then falling
back asleep
at six thirty am,

I wake to
the sound of chopping
timber,
the crying
of babies,
the thumping
of dozens
of bare feet
kicking a ball
outside,
and a little girl
with a whopping smile

smacking
her teeth
and winking
at me
over and
over again.

Foreign Language

As soon as I open
my eyes,
she runs away,
startled
and yelling
a phrase
I don't understand.

A Village of Faces

I step outside
and see
a large green field
filled with
twenty or
thirty boys
and girls
running,
kicking
a worn-out ball
between
two poles,
trying to
keep their balance.

A bell gongs
and the athletes,
along with
other kids who've
been milling around,
scurry
in military rows
like they're about
to be
inspected.

There must be a hundred

of them,
bright, little faces
all lined up
in front of the school,
smiling and silent.

What are they doing? I say to no one in particular.

I shrug my shoulders,
turn to head back inside,
gather my belongings
to figure out the next part
of my journey,
when they all start chanting,
GOOD MORNING, MR. BLADE.

I freeze.

To hear your name
called in unison
in a place
in a time
where you feel nameless
and alone
is as stunning
and shocking
as fireworks
on a Sunday
in December.

I turn back around,
to find Joy
waving me over.

Welcome

HOW ARE YOU? the children say, in unison.
HELLO! How are you?

We are fine, how are you?
I'm good.

Very nice to meet you, sir, they say, again in unison.
The children have a song they'd like to sing you, says
Joy, who's now standing next to me in front of all one
hundred children. *Children, are you ready?*

I am fully prepared for some traditional Ghanaian song,
but what I get is:

All the kids
doing *The Whip*
and *The Nae Nae*
in utter hilarity,
and one of the athletes
doing his best
Michael Jackson
impression,
moonwalk and all.

Stories

After about
an hour
of dance and song
and the kind
of cheer
I haven't had
in a while,
Joy introduces me
to a few children
who either want
a hug
or my ears
so they can tell me
their stories
their wishes
and the names
of their favorite
American pop stars.

I wish

to find
  my mother's
    reasons
      for leaving
        me alone
          and unsure
            that love
              exists.

Texts to Storm

3:30 pm
Now that I can scratch
sleeping in an African village
off my bucket list

3:30 pm
I'm going to a hotel
for a shower and a
Coke. Call me when

3:30 pm
you wake up,
sleeping beauty.

Goodbye

The taxi drivers
are plentiful now,
still arguing
over who gets
to drive
the American
to the nearest hotel.

The little, winking girl

with a smile
as big
as this country
and apparently
a voice
as powerful
as mine
comes screaming
and crying,
with Joy
chasing
behind her.

Mighty Protector

The little girl
hugs me tight, still crying,
and refuses to let go.

She thinks you are going to die, Joy says.
What? Why?

She says you were screaming in your sleep this morning.
Did I scare you with the mosquitoes? I'm sorry.
No, it wasn't that. I must have been dreaming again.

Well, Sia does not want you to leave. I think she wants to
protect you.
I see. That's so cute. But please tell her I have to go, that
I'm on a mission.

She is relentless. Plus, she sometimes stays with Auntie
Lucy. They are very close.
Is she an orphan?

She is.
. . . .

Sia, he must go, Joy says to the girl, whose tears have
paused since she reached my leg.
It's okay, I'll stay for a few extra hours, is what I really
don't want to say. But, I do.

Stay

Thank you for staying. You will be her world for the rest of the day.
It's no problem. She's a pretty cute kid.

We find
two folding chairs
near the school.

The sky is draped
in gray.
No rays of light,
but the little girl
dancing in front
of us
to the music
in her head.

When she finishes
entertaining us
she climbs
into my lap
and falls asleep.

Joy smiles. *See, that's all it takes.*

Conversation

So, where in America do you live, Blade?
Hollywood, California.

Ahh! The Land of Angelina Jolie and Brad Pitt.
Yep, the land of fake angels and broken wings.

What is your family like?
That is the last thing I want to talk about. Let's talk about you. Do you have a boyfriend?

I am too busy with my work for any boy.
Your work? What do you do?

I teach. I tutor. I cook. I help with the after-school art program. I help out in the village and, of course, at home.
How old are you?

Nineteen.
That's a lot of jobs. How do you do all that?

It's like asking "How do you wake up?" It's what I do. It's what I've done. I work.
But don't you want to live too?

She Tells Me

My work
begins
the moment
my eyes open
to the light.
I don't stop
until the night
pulls my eyelids
down like
warm blankets.
But I have fun
and sometimes
I sing.
So though I work,
I live.

Wait, you sing?

Conversation

I haven't had the time lately, but I used to go to Accra and
sing in a band with my mates.
What did you sing?

Rock and soul.
You mean rock and roll?

I mean Aretha Franklin.
That's soul music.

It's also rock.
I don't think so.

So Blade is also a Rock and Roll Professor?
Let's just say I know a lot about rock and roll.

I see. Do you know the first woman put into your Rock and
Roll Hall of Fame?
Hmm. Janis Joplin, maybe. Tina Turner?

Incorrect.
Really?

Really.
Who was it?

Aretha Franklin.
Get out!

It's true.
How do you know that?

Because you make me feel like a—
Natural woman, we sing, in harmony, and laugh.

Conversation

You sing too, huh?
A little. I used to play guitar. But I stopped.

Why?
Long story. I really want to hear you sing, though.

Ha! When you know me better, perhaps.
Can I ask you a question? What is my mother like?

*She is like you. American. Inquisitive. Kind. Pensive. Full
of wonder and wander. She says "I declare" a lot, like a
country singer. Do you know what it means?*
She's from Louisiana. It's how they talk. I guess it's like
an affirmation or surprise. Another way of saying, "That
is so cool!" Or, "I cannot believe that!"

Some of the kids are even saying it now!
Tell me, is she married?

That is something you will have to ask her.
Does she look like me?

*There is a resemblance. You walk the same. There is music
in your blood, Blade.*
. . . .

Country and western is her favorite kind of music.
No, it's not!

*Ha! . . . Tell me, Blade, why do you not play music
anymore?*

Why I Don't Play Music Anymore

It's what happens
when the sweetness
of life
turns sour
and putrid.
The innocence,
faith,
and trust
melts away,
evaporating
the good ole days
into a void.

I remember
not so long ago,
when I could make a girl
fall for me
by just playing
the strings.
When I could get
people to sing
and dance
around me
in ripples
and waves.

But the music died
inside of me
the day I
found out
my life,
my love,
was a lie.

The strings became
arrows
in my side,
killing me softly,
swiftly.

My life
no longer simple
and sweet
like American Pie.

My guitar
my love songs
my music
had to die.

That's why.

Confession

Everybody loves music, Blade. Music is story. It is the language of love and happiness.
Me and love have not gotten along too well; happiness is a foreign country, and my passport has expired.

This is why you've come to find your mother?
Part of the reason. It's also why I had to leave home and my helpless father. Betrayal was all around me.

Blade, your life sounds so unpromising.
It was. Funny thing is, I used to write a lot of love songs.

For whom?
A girl. A girl who I thought loved me.

She didn't?
She crushed me. And now love is like the sea closest to the horizon.

Offing.
Huh?

That is what it is called nearest the horizon.
You sure do know a lot, Joy.

I know that in order to receive it, you must give it, and that in order to give it, you must have it.
It?

Love.
Is that in the Bible or something?

It's in the heart, Blade.
Do you always talk like that?

What do you mean?
Like a sage or Gandhi or something.

You are funny, Blade.
I aim to please.

Before you leave, I should show you around, no?
That'd be cool.

What begins

as a tour of Konko
suspiciously becomes
an introduction
to village chores:

I chop wood
sweep dust and dirt
from the classroom floor
wash clothes
start a fire
try for an hour
to balance a bucket
on my head
filled only with
coconut leaves.

I must look like
a helpless clown
with axe stuck in log
and leaves on the ground.

The women who make it look
so simple chuckle,
but strangely, I'm happy
for the laughs,
for the stories
they share
about life and survival
and a history
never found in textbooks.

So, I try to fit in,
at least for a little while,
wishing I could belong
to something as simple

and as deep
as community.

Maybe it's the jetlag,
or the sleepless night,
or the fufu,
but something
is happening
to me.
These are not
the musings
of a teenager.
I'd give anything
for Rudy's ice cream
right now.
I'd give anything
for an argument
with Storm
or even Rutherford.

Purple Rain

My chores end
as do my hopes
for a shower
when the once indigo sky
turns a greenish-yellow
and suddenly opens
like it's another world
leaking into ours.

Thunderstorm

I hear
the sound
of God's hands
clapping
and watch
the storm pour
in sheets
so fast
and furious
I wonder
if this place
is going to
cave in.

I wonder
if I'm going to
cave in.
What am I even doing here?
I thought
I'd get some answers,
but the only thing
I'm finding
is more questions.

Back home,
when it would rain hard,
which was rare,
and Rutherford
was on tour,
Mom would drive
down Laurel Canyon Boulevard
to get us away
from mudslides
and the paparazzi.

We'd camp out
in Beverly Hills,
sometimes playing
in the pool,
getting wet
twice as much,
and laughing
'til we cried.

*Blade, the kids will want to play, but we need to get them
inside,* Joy says frantically. *The river is coming.*
What should I do with Sia? I ask.

*Watch her. Hold her. She loves the rain, and she's a fast
one.*

But it's too late,
she's darting beneath
the gushing monsoon,
giggling and
trapping raindrops
inside her smile.
So I join her.

Cleansed

We are drenched,
like Joy
and the other teacher,
who the kids
have tackled
in the rain.

We've all had
our baths
it seems,
yet somehow
Sia, the rowdiest
of them all,
has managed
to cover herself
in mud.

Rainy Season

Will taxis
still come? I ask
even though
I know
the answer.

*It will be difficult if the rain continues like this. So you will
stay here another night.*
I guess I don't have a choice. But, not in your all-purpose
room. That roof could cave any second if this keeps up.

You will stay with me and my uncle.
Thank you.

And it looks like we will have another guest as well, Joy
says, looking at Sia, who has attached herself to my leg
again.

I watch Joy

tend
to the children,
make sure each
reaches shelter.

I can't believe
she is almost
two years older
than me.

Serious, happy,
and cool
all at the same time.
Her name is fitting.

How did she end up
with so much wisdom
like the mountains
themselves created
her?

You are amazing, I say.
Ah, maybe you will write a song about me one day.

I don't think there are any more songs in me.
Of course there are. You just have to let the music find you.

Wordscram

The chicken stew
is not that bad.
I eat two bowls,
and after we clean up,
while Sia plays
with my phone,
Joy and I
play my favorite game.
for the last piece
of cake.

TR. Ten seconds. Ready, go!
Wait, that's too fast.

Fine, I'll start. Terrible Rains.
Hey, you stole mine.

Six seconds. Tick-tock.
Trouble Runner-Seeker.

That's three words.
I used a hyphen.

You can't make up your rules, Joy.
Aren't you running from trouble, but seeking?

Whatever, Thunderous Rebel-Rouser.
Ha! Transcontinental Roamer-Believer.

Tantalizing Rhythm-Keeper.
Who? Me?

Yes, You. The way you walk, it's, hmmm, mesmerizing.
Be careful, Blade. Timely Regrets.

. . . .
Your turn.

You win. Enjoy the cake.
Wahala!

Huh?
Means trouble. *Blade, you are Wa-ha-la!*

Texts to Storm

4:01 pm
Too busy to text your brother,
huh? No worries, I'm just
stranded in the middle of a

4:01 pm
monsoon in the Ghana
bush. Looks like another
night here. At least the food

4:01 pm
is decent. And I've met two
girls. Well, one is a little five-
year-old, who is the kind

4:02 pm
of sister I wish you were.
Kind, happy, not a nuisance.
Also, a very cute nineteen-year-

4:02 pm
old, who I think kinda
crushes me. But don't
all girls. I'm staying at

4:02 pm
her uncle's. He's old,
doesn't say a whole lot.
Better than last night's

4:03 pm
accommodations. I feel
a little helpless here. The
men spend their days cutting

4:03 pm
wood and building stuff,
which, as you know, I'm
no good at. I could write

4:03 pm
a song about it though,
if I had a guitar.
If I still played music.

4:04 pm
Kiss Mick and Jagger
for me. Hit me back,
Storm.

Bedtime

Enough texting. Time to rest.
Where will Sia sleep?

I suspect, in your arms.
I kinda need my space. Where do you sleep?

In the room in the back.
Can't she sleep with you?

Go on, ask her.

I look into Sia's eyes,
and nothing in them says
she is parting
with my arm, leg, or neck.
And then she winks,
as if to say,
Go on, I dare you,
break my heart.

Of course, you'll have to sing her a song.
Not gonna happen.

Or a story. Auntie Lucy always tells her stories.
I don't know any stories.

. . . .

I guess I could read her *Charlotte's Web.*

She won't fall asleep otherwise.
Is she potty trained?

She is five years, not five months. You will not have to
worry about that, Blade.
"Where's Papa," I read.

285

Alarm

You Americans sleep a lot, Joy says,
standing over me. *Wake up,*
my friend, let's eat.

Breaking Our Fast

We sit around,
and eat sweet bread
and fruit.

*Please, Sia, you need
to eat,* Joy begs.
*She thinks she can
live on stories
and song.*

I bet
I can get her
to eat something, I say.
Hey, Sia, watch this, and
I take
a piece
of bread
and gobble it
like a monster.

Sia giggles
and shoves
a piece of warm bread
and then another piece
into her mouth, then
gobbles it all
like a monster too.
Blade, we don't play with food, Joy says sternly, but
I can tell she
is trying
pretty hard
not to laugh.
Plus, she's happy
Sia is eating.

Joy says

when it rains
it pours
in Ghana.
There is no
safe passage
for teachers
to get
to school.
Craters
in the road
fill with water
and bathing birds,
and every inch
of earth
and sky
is blurred like
an impressionist
watercolor.
So there is no
school
and no
rules
for learning
until further notice.

Text to Storm

8:19 am
Morning. Still storming
here. I'm alive though, in
case you wondered. But,

8:19 am
my phone's about to die
because the electricity
just went out. Joy says

8:19 am
it happens regularly. WT??!!
She's cute. Joy. And smart.
Still crushing me. Holla back!

Holiday

Joy says we should
keep Sia on schedule.

Teach her
the alphabet,
read her a story,
help her learn
her chores.

But Sia wants to play games
and so do I.
So we run around
playing hide-and-seek
and then we crawl
on the floor
like mountain lions
on the hunt.

We growl
and laugh
then growl
some more.

You must think
this is holiday, don't you?
Joy says, shooting us
a look.

Sia and I get up
to dance
and Joy
hands us
a broom
and some rags
to start cleaning
her uncle's house.

Undeliverable

8:22 am
This is an auto-response.
The text message to Storm
Morrison failed to send.

Conversation

You move slowly without your little helper.
Is she coming back?

You will have your privacy now. She is off with a neighbor,
playing with cousins. She will be fine.
Oh.

You miss her already.
It's probably best. I really need to see my mother.

. . . .

. . . .

When you get back home, what will you do?
End of the summer, I'm off to college. You?

Eventually college. For now, I have responsibilities. Then, I
will save for my secondary studies.
You haven't finished high school yet?

I have one more year to complete.

. . . .

It costs one thousand dollars a year, and that is more than
most families here make in a year or two.
So no one goes to high school?

In the past ten years, only two have gone. Most of the girls
will become domestic helpers in the city, and the boys will
hunt and cut timber.
I'm sorry.

You should not be. There is work to be done here, to give
the people an opportunity, a world to build a life on. That
is nothing to be sorry about, Blade.

. . . .

After watching

her lips
spread
with such passion
and intent,
we share a moment
of silence
where I don't know
what to say
and I am staring
and the rain is dancing
and the moment feels perfect
for something.

The Moment

You know how
you can politely
be
at the tip
of a grand ocean
and you can see
the wave on its way
feel it propagating
through water
bending sprightly
toward
its crest

and

you know how
when she finally
spills
into you
pinnacles
and spindrifts
against your thrusts
and you are overcome
unbound
and nearly
engulfed?

That is how I feel
right
now
listening to
her speak.

Stare

Sorry. *What are you
thinking?* Family, I lie. *You've
hardly mentioned them.*

Family

What do you want to know about my house secrets? My family is an envelope that's sealed. Literally.
Well, there's a story in there. A before the envelope, a now, right? she says as rain pounds around us, keeping us inside, keeping us talking, and playing this guessing game of *who are you?*

Who am I? I don't really know, or I guess I don't really care.

I'm the son
of a man
who named me after
a Marvel Comic.

I'm the son
of an addict
who used to be
a guitar hero.

So that's where the music comes from.
The music has been with me since day one. Those guitar chords used to help me understand the world. There's always music in my head. Even still.

I can tell. You have a special rhythm when you walk and talk, she says, pinching my cheek. *Like your mother.*

She stares into my eyes.
I know this look.
This is the moment
of captivation.
I'm going in.

You know how
you can politely

be
at the tip
of a grand ocean
and you can see
the wave on its way . . .

What are you doing, Blade?

I was just . . . trying . . . to . . . kiss you.
Why?

Because it felt right.
That is not a good idea.

I thought we were vibing or something.
Chapel?

Huh?
Your arm. It's written in ink, with a rose.

. . . .
. . . .

She was my girlfriend. Emphasis on WAS!
I see.

. . . .

Blade, you can't just come kiss a girl because you miss a girl.

Someone I'm Trying to Forget

Her smell of spicy cinnamon
her golden skin a sunset
the blue wonder
in her gaze.

She could meld
into me,
and we would build
a tower
of love
that stood above
all the others:
the Empire, the Eiffel,
Liberty herself.

The city beneath us
wanted to see us crumble.
The lore of our love
had no choice
but to escape and
fall off . . .

She jumped
without me
leaving me
alone
without a light
and I've been lost since.

Conversation

You love your American woman.
I loved her.

Get some rest. I must check on the school and the families.
Wait, I'm sorry, Joy.

Don't be.
It won't happen again.

Blade, if there is no destination, why take the journey?

Thought

Her legs
her lips
are fire.
But, her goodness
could probably light my life,
if I weren't
such a shady secret.

After four days

of nonstop rain
electricity returns
and the sun
reveals itself,
finally.

The men
go back to cutting trees
the women wash
and balance
the world
on their heads.

The guide
returns tomorrow,
then I will make the trek
to Lucy November.

This is it.

Sia rejoins me,
under the coconut tree,
and we watch people.
I feel bad
that she has not
been in school,
so I teach her
counting, letters,
"Twinkle, Twinkle Little Star"
and every song
I can remember
Mom singing
to me
when I was little.

Conversation

Sia, Mr. Blade has to go to a hotel and get a proper shower.
Twinkle, twinkle, little star, she sings . . .

Exactly, but now I have to go.
Wonder what you are.

Give me a hug.
No, please, she says.

I will come back tomorrow and see you, before I go to
meet Lucy November.
Auntie Lucy, she says, her eyes big as the coconuts that
fall randomly.

Tomorrow, I finally get to meet her.
No, please. Bring Auntie Lucy. Don't go.

We hug each other,
and like a freight train,
a huge bus screeches to a halt
when an unmistakable voice
yells.

Rock 'n' Roll, Baby!

I look up and see
a familiar face
hanging
from the window
like a shaggy dog
dressed up
in glittered glam.
Like groupies
at a concert,
a motley crew—
guy with video camera,
biker woman with notebook, and
UNCLE STEVIE—
bounce
off the pimped-out bus,
making room
for their leader
to jump off
and tackle me
with a gold-
and-jewel-laden
bear hug.

Who is this? Sia asks.
Paapa, I answer in her language.

Paapa? she asks, looking at the strange man with the long
hair and the big guitar.
Yep, that is my father.

We're the Morrisons

Rutherford
just stands there
waving
at the children
like he's waiting
for applause.
He takes
his guitar
off his shoulder
and starts
jammin' right there
in the middle
of the village.
The children,
transfixed on the
pimped-out bus,
come running
from school
and swarm him
like he's the sweetest
thing they've never seen.
Even little Sia,
who hasn't left
my side
in days,
runs over
to him.

Conversation

Rutherford, what are you doing here?!
Don't act so surprised. We missed you, son!

You can't be serious!
*I'm clean. Got my sober coach, Birdie, who's helping
me stay on the straight and narrow, and my camera guy
filming me and Stevie's comeback.*

He adjusts all his rings
and bracelets and runs
his hands through his
unruly hair.

Comeback?
*Kid, the band is getting back together, and we got a
camera to document it. MTV, VH1, somebody's gonna be
all over this, son.*

Don't you think you should have called me before
showing up?
We did. Storm was in charge of that.

Delayed

My phone is barely charged,
and after four days
of no electricity
and spotty service,
I turn it on
to find two days
of incoming text messages
from my sister,
the last four
in ALL CAPS.

Texts from Storm

7:45 pm
BLADE, DAD AND UNCLE
STEVIE ARE COMING TO
GHANA IN THREE DAYS.

7:45 pm
TRIED TO STOP HIM, BUT
HE'S GOT A BIG IDEA. BE
NICE, BLADE. HE'S DOING

7:45 pm
BETTER. I WOULD HAVE
COME, BUT RECORDING.
HE RENTED A LUXURY

7:45 pm
PARTY BUS. GOOD
LUCK. WHY AREN'T YOU
RESPONDING TO MY TEXTS?

Conversation Continued

Being here for me doesn't mean being here for me in
Ghana. Go back to your castle, Rutherford.
*I want to be better. Now is my chance to grow and change.
Just like you. We have an opportunity to be better men,
Blade.*

Better men?
It'll be a wild reunion, he says, throwing up the peace
sign to the camera.

This is not cool. I put my hands in front of the camera
lens.
*We need to capture this for the masses. Fans need to see
our new and improved life. The good we're doing.*

We're doing?

The camera moves in closer.

GET THIS CAMERA OUT OF MY FACE.
*This, if we do it right, will be a reality show. Not scripted.
Real time. Real life. Don't worry if we look bad, they'll edit
it out.*

YOU NEED TO CUT THIS OUT, RUTHERFORD.
You can't just come here and interrupt these people's
lives.
*I think it would be good for fans to see us helping these
little village people in Ghana. Imagine that, Blade. The
Morrisons saving lives. We can build something or buy
something. Did you get that*, he says to the camera guy.
That was authentic sh—

Are you KIDDING me? You want to walk into this
village like a rock 'n' roll savior and call these people
"little village people." You are an insult to humanity. You

309

don't know them. Please leave.
NOW!

Rutherford puffs out
his chest, stands
two inches
from my face.

*I flew all the way here for this. Don't be ungrateful. Your
mother would want us doing this. You and me together.*
Oh, you're going to bring up Mom now?

*Don't make the show start off with a brawl between me
and you.*
Why not? It'd be good for TV, right? Isn't that what you
want?

That actually wouldn't be a bad thing, the camera guy
says, adjusting his lens.
They'll be none of that, Uncle Stevie says to him. *Kid,
your father—*

Look, I don't care what y'all do, but you're not going to—
But before
I can finish,
Joy walks up
and wedges herself
between us.

Please, no fighting in front of the children, she says,
shaking her head. *Grown men want to wrangle like little
boys. Let's talk this out over coconut.*

Introductions

I've heard a lot about you, Mr. Guitar Hero, Joy says,
laughing and shaking his hand.

She hands us each
a coconut half
with a straw
inserted.

*I am honored to be here to capture the untapped beauty
and potential that is Ghana.*
Don't you mean to exploit the beauty and potential, like
you do with everything else?

Blade, we are respectful of our elders.
Wait, I'm not an elder. I'm your super soul brother, he
says, winking at Joy, who, for some reason, is egging him
on. *It's lovely to meet you, Joy,* he says, kissing her hand.
*This glorious day is made even more enchanting by your
obvious pulchritude.*

I can see where your son's charm comes from.
I can see why Blade is smitten with you.

What are you talking about?
It's written all over your face.

Plain as a naked jailbird, Uncle Stevie chimes in.
*Thank you, Mr. Morrison . . . It has been a blessing to
meet your son. He has a lot he's searching for.*

So, where's the mystery woman? He signals to the camera
guy. *Hey, make sure you get this. I'm about to meet my
son's mother.*
That's why you're here? You're a real piece of work,
Rutherford. Well, you're outta luck, 'cause she's not here.

No worries, we'll just shoot me interacting with the villagers. Ya know, you could really be a shining star for the camera, Joy.

You can't bring a camera here to the village without permission.
It's all right, Blade, we are used to Americans and their cameras. But you must meet the elders tomorrow, Mr. Morrison. They will decide the fate of you and your camera.

Joy gathers
our empty
coconut halves.

You gentlemen behave, she says,
leaving us
alone, unsure.

Way to go, Rutherford.
You can get us kicked
out of
an entire country now
instead of
a hotel.

Rutherford gives

a tour
of his air-conditioned
satellite TV
pimped-out bus
with bunk beds
to anyone
who is interested,
which is practically
everyone
in the village,
especially Sia,
who jumps on
Rutherford's bed
and refuses
to leave.

Joy asks me
to pick Sia up
and carry her out,
but when I try
she wails
like I'm
a monster
come to gobble her up.

I guess it's a slumber party, he yells, picking Sia up and
swinging her around.
Fine with me, if you're okay, Blade, Joy says.

Do you really trust two foreigners with this innocent
child?
Look how far you've come. Look where you both are.
Father and son. I trust that you are capable. Are you not?

. . . .

Do not worry, Blade. She will be fine. I will see you in the
morning.

Twinkle, Twinkle

After playing
peek-a-boo,
hide-and-seek,
and Uno
with Rutherford,
she dozes off
on a bunk bed
in my arms
to the rock version
of her now favorite
song.

Luxury

I despise this bus.
Don't want to be on this bus.
It's everything
I left.
But she's here,
sleeping
in the middle
of his
corrupt,
unpredictable,
ungodly excess.

Her breathing
rises and falls
like the cadence
of soft music.

I crack open
Track by Track,
read it
by the light
of my phone
for the umpteenth time
because it brings me closer
to Mom's stardust,
to a little bit of peace
in the darkest of nights
no matter where I am.

Track 9: It's Only Love (LIVE)

ROCKERS: TINA TURNER AND BRYAN ADAMS / ALBUM: *TINA LIVE IN EUROPE* / LABEL: CAPITOL / RECORDING DATE: 1985–1987 / VENUE: VARIOUS CONCERTS

Mom always said
"It's Only Love"
is the greatest
rock duet
of all time,
and if aliens
ever landed,
it would be
the song
she'd play
to greet them.

Why? I asked her.

Because of the energy.
The passion in it
gets you
through the
hard times
sad times
mad times.
Doesn't matter
if someone disappoints you,
if they hurt you,
it's never the end
of the universe.
Remember that, Blade.
It's only love,
she'd say,
and give me

a bear hug
and butterfly kisses.

But don't forget,
she'd also remind me,
love is everything too.

Freak Show on Wheels

Uncle Stevie's snoring
sounds like
a garbage disposal
and the camera guy
wheezes.
Rutherford still talks
in his sleep.
It's like a nightmare band
and I'm the audience
wishing this freak show
was over.

So I get up, stretch my legs, see if they've got any snacks
around here.

*The butter cookies are so good. But they're addictive. I'm
on number eleven.*

. . . .

*Sorry, didn't mean to startle you. We haven't been formally
introduced. I'm Birdie.*
Blade.

*Nice to meet you, Blade. Your father's told me much about
you.*
You're his new one.

I'm his new sober coach.
Of course you are.

Sober coaches

make a killing
keeping rockers
and movie stars
alive
'round the clock.

Birdie claims
she makes sure
Rutherford stays centered,
doesn't get lit,
go out on a bender.

Says she's here
to rip
the drugs or whiskey
straight out
of his mouth and hands
if necessary.

Follow him around
like a stalker
and get paid
beaucoup loot
to listen,
offer advice,
and just sit
and stare
at him.

Conversation

Your father's an alcoholic with a drug problem.
Duh?

I'm here to help him.
No disrespect, but been there, done that.

You have any questions for me?
Yeah, have you checked his boot?

And his socks, and his guitar case, and every inch of his
suitcase.
. . . .

I watch. I wait. I listen.
And all the world watches and listens too, I say, pointing
to the camera on the tripod, even recording his sleep.

*Not my idea. They think the camera is their ticket back to
glory.*
They're delusional.

Maybe, maybe not. I've seen worse come back.
Yeah, okay . . . How long's he been clean?

*I'm not really at liberty to discuss his treatment and
recovery with anyone, not even his son.*
So what, like a day?

*I'm here because he's serious about this road to recovery.
He knows it's his one last chance to make it up to you.*
Sounds desperate.

I'll tell you this; deep down, he's a good guy.
They all are.

*He is. He struggles every single day. He craves. Look at
him over there. All the sweating is not just from this heat.*
. . . .

He's got a lot of love for you and your sister.
Love?

Yes, Love. Love is complicated all around—twisted humanness, flaws and scars so deep, it would take an excavator to dig out the meaning of it all.
I guess.

You should rest.
I really don't want to be here. This is just like him. All this excess. I just want to be gone.

Then go.
. . . .

You love him, you'll support him.
Who's gonna support me? I'm a little sick and tired of supporting him only to have him skip out on rehab, or relapse. What's the point? It never sticks.

I think if he has the will and the support of his loved ones and a killer sober coach, he could be free.
I just don't know if I believe it. I've been disappointed too many times.

Give him a shot. In the meantime, I've eaten way too many butter cookies. I'm going to sleep. You should too. But first, hit the shower. You're a little funky.
Shower?

Perplexed

How Rutherford got
a tour bus
in Ghana
with four bunk beds
a pullout sofa
a fish tank
and satellite TVs
I cannot begin
to fathom,
but the fact
that there's a shower
makes my life
right now.

Texts to Storm

1:01 am
I'm pissed at you
because your warning came
a day late, and a dollar

1:01 am
short. Phone and Wi-Fi
service here sucks! I got
your messages after

1:02 am
the rolling stone had
already shown up. So,
I guess, thanks for nothing.

1:02 am
It's a nightmare. And, I
haven't even met her yet.
The whole reason I'm

1:02 am
even here, and I keep
getting these roadblocks.
I can't get no flippin' satisfaction.

Delayed

1:03 am
This is an auto-response.
The text message to Storm
Morrison was delayed.

The next morning

I look out
the window
and see Rutherford
and Uncle Stevie
kicking soccer balls
with the kids
as the camera
and Birdie
watch.

Unsettling

On the walk
to school
Sia suddenly
starts gagging,
then lets go of
my hand
and throws up
all over
my flip-flops.

I carry her
back to
the bus
to rest,
but halfway there
we hear
a pulsing wave
of music,
a loud, fast tremolo
coming
from the school,
so we turn around
and she jumps down,
leading me
back to
a very familiar sound.

Captured

The entire school
of students
and teachers
plus people
in the village
are gathered
in the church SLASH school
cheering
and watching
as Rutherford Morrison
drops electric bombs
in the air
like he's Jimi Hendrix
and Konko
is Woodstock.

Track 10: The Star Spangled Banner (LIVE)

ROCKER: JIMI HENDRIX / DATE: AUGUST 18, 1969 / VENUE: WOODSTOCK MUSIC AND ART FAIR, WOODSTOCK, NY

Rutherford said
his dad
once saw Jimi
play the guitar
with his teeth,
and that he actually
set his guitar
on fire once,
which helped
set his career
on fire.
But most people agree
that the defining
moment
in Jimi Hendrix's life
was when he
stood on stage
in a blue-beaded
leather jacket
with a red scarf
at the Woodstock Music
and Art Fair
in front of
40,000 people
after being awake
for three days,
and played
an amped-up,
distorted,

electric guitar solo
of "The Star Spangled Banner,"
which the editors of
Guitar World
called
the number one
greatest performance
ever.

EVER!

Music Lessons

When he finishes,
all the kids
want to know
how to play
the strings,
make the guitar sing
and reverb
like he just did.

Sia
climbs
into his lap
touches his face
and traces
the lines
on his forehead
and cheeks.

Old, she says.

He tickles her
in a way I remember
him doing to me
and Storm
a long time ago.
He allows Sia
to strum the guitar,
gets the kids
pumped up
with a hope
he'll never
be able to fulfill.

This, I know.

Conversation

Are you jealous of your father? Joy asks.
No, I just don't want him to get their hopes up.

That is what they need, to have their hopes up.

. . . .

You seem distracted.
I'm angry. It shouldn't be this hard. I just want to meet
my mother. I JUST WANT TO GET OUT OF HERE
AND FIND HER.

*I understand. I'm sorry that it's not easier. Sometimes the
things that are good in life take work. And patience.*
I've been patient. I'm almost eighteen years old, and I
have no idea what I'm doing. Being here doesn't even
make sense anymore. I thought I could escape the
madness, but it just followed me. I can't stay here. I'm
going to find her on my own.

The Elders

Five men
with graying beards
and one woman
in a colorful kente dress
sit in
a circle
allowing
Rutherford Morrison
to charm them
into letting him
interrupt
their lives
with his annoying camera
and reckless attitude.
They applaud
his empty promises
of reality TV fame,
welcome
his Hennessy
and iPad gifts,
and wish him
well in his
rock 'n' roll comeback.

But, Dad, what about the dormitory? I ask, loud enough
for everyone to hear me, even the elder who was nodding
off. Didn't you say you would build a dormitory for the
teachers, with a cafeteria and showers for everyone in the
village to use?
*The gentleman will build a dormitory, so that the rains will
not halt school*, the one woman present echoes, standing
up and clapping as the other elders follow suit.

At first, he is silent, then he kinda nods his head, looks at the camera, and says, *Yes, I will build it. I will build the best dormitory possible for the village of . . . of . . .*
Konko, says the camera guy.

And for the first time since he's arrived, I laugh.

Acting

If that's the price I gotta
pay to regain your trust
and love, I'll pay it, he says,
giving me a hug
right in front
of the camera.

All day

in the burning sun,
the camera is in
our faces
like an invader
from planet
Hollywood.

I try to ignore, but
it captures
every word,
each drop of sweat,
every bite of food.

A little obnoxious while we feed our faces, don't you
think? Can we take a break from the filming now?

He pops up
zooms in
and out
as Rutherford,
Birdie, and Uncle Stevie
prance around
like the Three Stooges
leading a parade
of innocents.

By day's end

the camera
is still here
along with
the last streams
of sunlight
to close out the day,
and the kids
can't get enough.

The smiles
on their faces
as they perform
for the camera,
singing, twirling, dancing,
and jumping around
say it all:
happiness, raw like
unfiltered honey.

They ask for playbacks
so they can
see themselves
for the first time.

They hover
around
camera guy's monitor
and watch
their lives
unfold in laughter
and hugs.

Mirrors

The kids act like they've never seen themselves. Don't
you have mirrors here?
*Why do we need mirrors when we can see the reflection of
our goodness in the way others react to us?*

Seriously, sometimes you need to check out your hair or
make sure you don't have food in your teeth.
*Look at the mirrors in your friends' eyes. That's all anyone
ever needs. To see beauty and reflection in others. Those
are real mirrors.*

Okay, I get it.
*You are so gullible, Blade. Of course we have mirrors—
well, most of us do,* she says, laughing.

But it made sense.
Of course it did. Two things can be true at the same time.

Then she gets close
to my face,
and in her eyes
I see my reflection.
It's surprisingly happy
for the first time
in a while.

C'mon, Elvis is back.
Elvis?

The guide. It seems he is back just in time for you to leave.

In their language

Elvis
tells Joy
that my mother
is still
in the mountains
and that he will
go back in five days
if it does not rain,
and, yes,
the American
can come
along.

Thank him, Joy, I say, but I am not waiting five days. Can
you please ask him if he'd be kind enough to accept cash
to take me tomorrow? Please?

Game Night

Another night
of music
and games—this time
Sia and I
play Freeze
and Hot Potato—
but the highlight
for her
is the tickle fight
she and Rutherford
have, that leaves him
passed out
on the bunkbed
and me
and Joy
laughing so hard
we decide
to go for a walk.

People Are People

Two hundred dollars is more than a kind gesture. I will ask Elvis to accept half.
That's not necessary. I just want to get on with this. I'm tired of waiting.

. . . .

. . . .

Are you nervous?
Very. But I'm excited too. This is finally happening.

I'm happy for you. I am glad you came here.
Me too.

Your father does not need to build us a dormitory, please tell him that.
He seems serious, and, I mean, you do need it.

How do I say this without sounding ungrateful?
Huh?

The people who come here to help never ask us what we need. They tell us.

. . . .

One church started the school, another promised to fix it. One group built two wells, but didn't leave any tools or show us how to repair it.
That's why you have to walk so far for water?

I am appreciative. We are all appreciative. These things help us, but it would be nice to be asked sometimes what we want.
What do you want?

A stove would be nice. Perhaps, a washing machine, she says, laughing.
Really?

340

The women spend half of the day washing clothes. There is no time for their own self-development. There is no time to help their children with homework. We are so busy cleaning.
I see.

Maybe I will come visit you in America one day.
That would be nice.

Blade, there is something I must tell you. There are some whose eyes grow big at the sight of cash. They see your father as a treasure chest, and they think Konko has struck gold.
What does that mean?

People are people everywhere, Blade. We have gold diggers here too.
I like you, Joy. I think I—

Good night, Blade, she says, and it's only then,
when she lets go
of my hand,
do I realize
I've been holding hers
for the last ten minutes.

I wake up

to a familiar song
sung by
a hundred
little perfect voices
and one screaming
guitar.

Hey, kid, get up, it's your big day, Uncle Stevie says,
hitting me with a pillow.

Standing outside

the bus
is a washed-out rock star
with a five-year-old angel
on his shoulder
and a
multitude
of shining sons
and daughters
drumming
dancing
and singing.

For me.

Happy Birthday

On the one hand,
I'm probably
the only kid
on earth
who forgot
his eighteenth birthday.

On the other,
can you really blame me
for not being eager
to celebrate
eighteen years of
not knowing
who made me

or why?

A Gift Returned

Rutherford hands
Sia to me,
climbs
into the bus
and shouts . . .

Be right back. Nobody move!

Then reappears
with
a guitar.
A fancy new one.
He walks over to me
like he's gonna
serenade me.

Another one to add to your collection, huh? I ask.
Not my collection. This one's for you.

It looks like
it dropped
from heaven.
The sexiest acoustic-electric guitar
I've ever seen.

This had Blade written all over it, he says to me.
I don't know what to say.

Well, you could start by saying, Sorry I crushed that
priceless Van Halen, Dad.
I don't, I mean, I—

Kid, this is pure Madagascar rosewood. Rare as love. Just
thank him, and play something, Uncle Stevie says.
Thank you.

It's beautiful; what are you going to play? Joy says,

knowing full well, I won't.
It's nice, but I'm not really . . . I mean—

Play, play, Sia interrupts, getting louder with each echo.
PLAY!

I take the guitar
from Rutherford,
before she starts
breaking my heart
with her tears.

Maybe later, I lie, letting her pluck the strings.

But it does feel good
to hold
a guitar
again.

Sure, I've missed

the love songs
and the memories
embedded
in the strings.

The weight
of comfort
in my arms.

The feel
of the tuning keys
twisting
between fingers.

The blue-streak buzz
of voltage vibrating
in my head.

That was the guitar
I loved.

How many days has it been?
How many hours of longing
for the purple haze
to find me
again.

But this. Now.
I don't think so.

I've lost my chance
to get
the spark back.

Before I leave

we eat sweet butter
cake
from a bakery

in town
and play more games.
Sia runs

in and out of
a tower of legs,
chasing me.

Chasing Rutherford.
Climbing
my back

and his
like we're mountains
or trees.

She braids
and twists
his long,

outrageous hair.
Rubs her fingers
in mine,

reminding me
of happy times.
I will miss her.

When We Were Younger

Sometimes,
on special occasions,
at the end
of a show,
Rutherford
would bring me
and Storm on stage
in front of
tens of thousands
of screaming fans
and introduce us
as his little
superheroes.
Then he would
let her sing
any song
she wanted:
"Twinkle, Twinkle,"
"This Little Light,"
and while she
wailed, mostly off-key,
he'd strum,
with his right hand,
a melody for her.
And with his left,
he'd massage
my head,
which was his way
of saying *I love you*
and *Everything's*
gonna be okay.
I believed him,
despite

all our madness.
And, I guess
I still do.

Track 11: With or Without You

ROCKERS: U2 / ALBUM: *THE JOSHUA TREE* / LABEL:
ISLAND / RECORDING DATE: JANUARY 1986–JANUARY 1987 /
STUDIO: DANESMOATE HOUSE, DUBLIN, IRELAND

A haunting
aching song
about the complex
tangled vines
that leave you
feeling twisted
and crazy,
yet connected
and unable
to let go
of the possibility
that one day
the vines will
produce flower
or fruit
or something worth
all the pain.

Rutherford and I
have been
twisted
into a knot of
our own making
for so long
that I don't even
know if I can
loosen up.

Parting

Happy Birthday, Blade, Joy says, handing me a red-black-
and-gold hand-stitched bangle with my name on it.
Thank you, Joy. This is so cool! One of your many
talents?

I suppose.
I will never take it off.

Remember me by it.
It's not like I'm leaving forever. I've got to come back this
way.

I know. I guess we're just used to you. Are you packed?
Just a backpack.

You will not admit it, but you're happy he's here, she says.

I'm happy,
when he's sober
and clean

when he's kind
and generous
with the children

when he's a father
and puts us before
the addiction
of fame

when he shreds
the guitar
like a madman

and gives everything
to the music.

When he belts out
songs
in my mother's honor

and shows me
that quitting this life
is not an option.

Yeah, that's when I'm happy, I reply.

Words

Most of the children here
speak better English
than us,

and Sia really seems
to be interested in learning
as many words

as she can consume.
I teach her
brave

and *smart,* then hug
her goodbye
without saying it.

Rutherford teaches her
reverb and rock
and *Fender.*

She teaches us
to count to ten
in native tongue.

But what does your name mean, Sia? Rutherford asks,
as she runs off
with one of his
bawdy gold chains.
And he chases her wildly,
both of them
going nowhere
in particular, and
everywhere
at the same time.

What does her name mean, Joy?
It means "to help."

They return

moments later
with Birdie
cradling Rutherford
in one arm
and holding Sia
in the other.
He's sweating,
which is not unusual
given that it's
95 degrees,
but he's shaking too,
which is unusual
given that it's
95 degrees.

Let's get him inside the bus, Birdie says.
Why? What's happening?

Withdrawal

I've seen this before.
Many times.

Once the alcohol
and drugs
start leaving
the system,
the sweats
the sleeplessness
and dry heaves
kick in.

Rutherford craves,
rocks
back and forth,
fighting off
a demon
that lives
in his body
that whispers
temptation
in his mind.

Conversation

I've done this a million times. He just has to want it. But I'm working with him, Birdie says.

. . . .

He called me five days ago. He was really in a bad way.

. . . .

You're not saying much.
Not much to say, is there . . . Looks like I'm still stuck here.

Detox

Only after Sia
falls asleep
is Joy able
to take her
off the bus
so Rutherford
can rest.

How long do you think it will be, Birdie?
He'll hallucinate, he'll vomit, he'll have fitful sleep, if any
at all. This could take several days. Hard to tell. He's been
through this a lot, I bet.

That's an understatement.
I'll make sure it sticks.

Don't make promises you can't keep.
We got his back, says Uncle Stevie.

How about we turn off the camera?
He told me to keep filming, no matter what.

Yeah, but, this is different—
He's right, Birdie says. *Rutherford told him, keep shooting,*
or he won't get paid.

Fine.
I'm catching some zzz's, Uncle Stevie says, climbing into
the bunk.

I watch Rutherford
toss and turn,
restless as rain
and wonder
if I'll
ever get out of

this squall
that owns my life
and if I'll ever
get to her.

Cursed

Each time
I get closer
to meeting
the woman who
brought me
into this world,
something stops me
dead in my tracks.
"Pick up a guitar
and you'll be cursed,"
is the old joke
told in my house.
But, there's nothing funny
about this truth.

I am.

I pluck

a few strings
at a time,
like a beginner

beginning again,
strumming
a few chords

here and there,
my fingers crawling
up and down

my new guitar
like I'm trying
to remember.

Diving Back In

After warming up
a few long minutes,
the pain creeps in.
It settles inside like an old friend,
but so does the glory
of knowing I'm good
at something
that can't die on me
if I don't let it.

So I dive in,
really dive into the strings
like a skydiver freefalling
into the music,
and it kinda feels like a new
life could be beginning.
But I'm not sure.

A day later

he's finally
asleep.

My fingers
start to cramp,
but it feels
like the right
kind of pain.

I've missed this.
Feeling
every fiber
in my body
vibrate
to the rhythm.

I miss this.
Freedom.

Over the next

three days
Birdie comforts
and feeds
Rutherford.

I haven't been
this close
to him
this long
since . . .

never.

Storm calls
and speaks
to him,
which makes
him smile
through watery eyes
in between
the delirium
tremens.

Joy checks
on us periodically,
brings us
stews and soups
and joy.
She gives me
a message
that sounds nice
coming from
her lips,
even though
it's Sia's words:

Ma wifo. It means "I miss you."

On the fourth day

I wake
to the laughter
of Rutherford, Sia, and
a dozen kids
standing over me.

Sia holds
a mirror
to my face,
which is painted
like Gene Simmons
from KISS.

Rutherford shouts out, *Rock and Roll All Nite, BABY!*
Very funny. Very funny, I shout, chasing them off the
bus, relieved that things are back to normal.

Whatever normal is.

The Duo

Before Rutherford arrived
it was all about me.

Now Sia and Rutherford
are a band.

They play together.
They eat together.

They laugh together.
They crash together.

They prank together.
They are happy together.

Texts from Storm

5:19 am
Dad sounds better.
Please take care of him,
Blade. He's our only

5:19 am
father. Well, mine at
least. Just kidding! Seriously,
though, when are you going

5:20 am
to meet your mother? Can
you hurry up and do that,
so y'all can come home?

5:20 am
I miss you two. Mick
and Jagger miss you
too. Chapel called me

5:20 am
yesterday. I told her
you met someone new.
A model from Africa. She

5:21 am
was JEALOUS! LOL!
Hey, you like the new guitar?
I helped him find it.

5:21 am
And, can you please tell
me about Ghana, besides
it's beautiful and you're

5:22 am
in love. Like, try using
an adjective or two.
And, send pics. Hugs!

Texts to Storm

1:21 pm
He's doing better.
Back to his old antics.
Birdie definitely has him

1:21 pm
on a leash. She's like
a hawk. Uncle Stevie
pretty much sleeps

1:21 pm
all the time. Stomach
issues. He can't handle
the food. Haven't seen

1:22 pm
the camera guy very much,
which is really good
or really bad. Not sure.

1:22 pm
She's not a model, stupid.
But, we're just friends.
Don't mention C@#!? again.

1:22 pm
You want me to
describe Ghana, huh?
Fine, how's this . . .

Konko

is a village
of brown and green
apron of Mother Earth
gray, puffy sky—
a temperamental sea
that swallows
that keeps me looking and laughing
to the clouds— Today
I saw a sign
near a small lake
that read: No Drowning.

Red and green
buckets of
water travel
miles
suspended
in air
to glorious rhythms
of routine
under hidden sun
of orange fiery promises.

The smiles here
are abundant,
a crest of waves
across faces
young and old
that fly
with wings
of kings and queens
in search of
trees rooted
in ancient ground

history with arms
that reach
and give and give
crowns of flowers
and coconut milk,
the ambrosia
feeding my
wandering soul—it's brought
the music back to me.

Most gatherings are here
under the big coconut tree.
This place, covered in
brilliant sun
and humbling moon,
captures joy
in song and dance
of women and men
happy to be
singing
and
alive
with sounds
that never sleep,
past the magic
dust dreams.

Here, I can lift
my hands
into sky
pull down
the promises,
into my palms.

In other words, this place is beautiful, Storm . . .

Text from Storm

2:09 pm
Chills.

Conversation

How's Storm?
She's good. Says hello.

Can I join you?
Been a free country since 1957.

You like this place.
It's cool. A lot realer than Hollywood.

Yeah, I like it too. It's poor, though, kinda sad.
It's rich in ways you and your camera can't see.

You never gonna cut me any slack. That's the Morrison in
you. My dad was like that.
Thing is, I'm not a Morrison.

You are in my book, and I'm proud of you, son.
Save it. So proud you never told me I was adopted? Who
lies to their child like that?

Sunny thought—
There you go, trying to bring Mom into it again.

She loved you like her own. We loved you like our own.
Blood or no blood. We were young and stupid. We just
didn't think—
That's the problem, you didn't think.

. . . .

. . . .

We were gonna tell you. On your eighteenth birthday.
That's why she wrote the letter. Did you read it?
No.

You should read it.
I don't know.

There are some things in there she wanted you to know.
What about what I want? Did you ever consider that?

Always.
You're lying. I WANTED to grow up in a house with
a dad who didn't leave a string of nannies to raise us.
Who didn't come in wasted when he was in town. Who
wasn't plastered all over the tabloids for God knows
what. What I WANTED was not having to spend every
night worrying if you were gonna be arrested or end up
in some hospital. Do you know how tough it was to not
know whether your parent was gonna die? Do you know
how many nights Storm cried herself to sleep?

. . . .

You know what, it doesn't even matter. I just hope you
can last until you bail on these folks. They don't deserve
any of it.

*You're right. I just never learned how to live, how to, uh, be
without her,* he says, then he gets all teary-eyed, and I feel
like the bad guy. *I'm trying to do the right thing, I really
am, Blade. I just miss her.*
Yeah, well, we all do, but I already lost one parent—I
don't want to lose another.

Now he's full on crying,
and I probably should
hug him or something,
but before
I get the nerve
to do just that,
his ace,
our little princess
Sia,
comes running
up to him,

374

starts wiping his tears
and winks at him,
repeatedly,
which, of course,
makes us both howl
with laughter.

*I'm gonna make it, Blade. I'm gonna beat this. I promise
you. And, if there's anything I can do to prove to you that
you mean more to me than anything, other than Storm
and this little snickerdoodle,* he says, picking Sia up and
swinging her around. *Just name it.*
There is one favor I need . . .

While he teaches

Sia the words
to "Stairway to Heaven"
under the coconut tree,
she begins to vomit,
then cries
a helpless cry.

Rutherford throws down
the guitar,
looks at me
with horror
in his eyes
like he's never seen
a kid puke.

Is she okay?
IS SHE OKAY?
Where is the nurse?

She is fine. We will take care of her, one of the nearby
women in the village says,
picking Sia up, and whisking her away.
What happened to her? he asks Joy.

I think you should teach her a different song the next time,
she responds, laughing.
She'll be okay?

She will, Mr. Morrison. She will rest from all the activity.
Like you probably should.

. . . .

Sunday Night

Rutherford calls a meeting.

Life is too short, he exclaims to me, Joy, Uncle Stevie,
Birdie, and the camera dude. *We gotta climb the highest
mountain, swim the widest sea . . . before we turn to earth.
I wanna do something. Big. Memorable.*
*Yeah, because if we really think we have a shot at selling
this reality show, we definitely need more OOOOHS
and AHHHHS,* says the camera guy, smiling behind his
camera.

*Let's bring the rock and the roll, but, uh, what exactly
are you talking about, Morrison?* says Uncle Stevie,
whose stomach is back to normal—which everyone can
appreciate, since the ventilation on the bus is a little
limited.
*Birdie insists I need to exercise, that it will help my body
heal from all the toxins. So, we're going with Blade.*

With Blade? Where?
To find his mother. We'll climb Kilimanjaro, if we have too.

Kilimanjaro is in East Africa, camera guy says.
No, you're not. I'm doing this alone. I don't ne— I don't
want you there.

It's a seven-hour trek, Mr. Morrison, are you sure you can—
Joy says.
*You don't think I can handle it. I may be fifty, but I feel
nineteen,* he says, winking at her. *But, will there be a
mountain for us to climb?*

*Yes, there is a mountain, plus canopies, plus forest, before
we reach the village.*
A canopy? Like a suspension bridge or something? asks the
camera guy, who puts the camera down for the first time.

Yes, says Joy. *A provisional bridge. It was built by the Dutch. Maybe four hundred feet above.*
Above what? he asks, looking as frightened as I feel.

Look, you aren't going. This is not happening. Birdie, he needs the rest. Tell 'em.
It is kind of long, Rutherford . . . On the other hand, a little workout will build the endorphins. To heck with it, let's all sweat it out.

Then, it's settled. We head out at first light. Oh, this is going to rock! Rutherford hollers.
And roll, Uncle Stevie chimes in.

Uh, I think I'm gonna be sick, says the camera guy.
I'll double your pay for the day.

I think I'll be just fine, he says, picking the camera back up.
Quick question, Joy. Can we bring Sia?

Worth the Chance

Wait up, please, she says, grabbing my arm.
Sorry. I can never get away from him fast enough.

You are very upset. I understand.
This is a disaster. He can't be with me. This is not about
him.

It is a little. It is about your whole family, is it not?
You're taking his side? He's the one who's been lying to
me.

Sometimes a lie is kinder than the truth.
Kinder for him.

*You could give him a chance. Your heart may not feel it,
but it will catch up.*
He's screwed up everything. My graduation. My
girlfriend. My music. My life.

Blade, you cannot build a house for last year's summer.
. . . .

*Perhaps you should look to the future. Start over with him.
Your father might surprise you. Is that not worth it?*
. . . .

*Plus, I could go too. You will need my protection from the
mountain lions.*
I'm not falling for that again.

We are friends, aren't we?
Yes.

*Then trust me. It will be fine. You and he will be better for
it.*
. . . .

So you say yes?
I say I hope all this chaos is worth it.

All that is good and accomplished in this world takes work
and a little chaos.
Sia's not going to take it too well that we're leaving.

She's in no condition to travel with us.
Is she getting better?

They will take her to the doctor in town while we are gone.
She'll be okay though, right?

She will be in good care.

She lets go of my arm
and walks ahead like
she owns the road
and all the moxie
the world's created.

The next morning

we try
to convince
a fragile Sia
to eat
her porridge,
but she just cries,
begs to come
with us, does not
understand that
she needs
to stay
and rest
so we can play
more pranks,
more card games,
when we return.

We try
to convince her
that this is only
a trip
for old rockers
trying to be better,
that she's our
shining princess, and
when that doesn't work,
one of the women
caring for her
scoops her up,
takes her
off the bus
kicking
and screaming.

Will she be okay? Rutherford asks.

She is being a child. You have spoiled her, Joy replies, but there is some worry in her eyes.

She deserves to be spoiled, he answers. *And there'll be more of it when we return. But right now, onwards. Let's go shout our names atop a mountain.*
Yes. Elvis waits for us, Joy says. *Onwards!*

9:15 am

Rutherford loads
the Mercedes van
he's rented
for the trip
He holds up his guitar
like he's offering it
to the sun.

May the force be with us!

On the way,
Elvis listens
to talk radio
that features
nonstop
belligerent
banter
that only he
and Joy understand,
for the most part,
except every
few minutes
when an expletive
English word
is sprinkled in,
followed by
garish laughter.
So, the rest of us
try to sleep.

Anxiety

The van flies,
rattles across
heavily potholed roads
bringing me closer
to my mother,
but it can't catch
up to my brain,
which is speeding
past me.
Running
running fast
running past
shadows and
blurred trees
and before
and now
and if I could catch up
to my thoughts,
wrestle them
to the ground,
tame them inside
the cage
of my head,
I could breathe.
I could breathe
I COULD

Breathe, Blade. Breathe, Rutherford says, rubbing my
head, and looking at me with eyes that care. *It's gonna be
okay. Just breathe.*

11:09 am

A few hours into
the bumpy drive
we arrive at a
parking lot
where hundreds
of cars and vans
are in a standstill
traffic jam.
Thousands of women,
boys, and girls
peddle
toys, bags of water,
and bracelets
like the one
Joy made for
my birthday.

I glance over
at her, and notice
that she even smiles
when she sleeps.

Not polite to stare, she says, her ebony and ivory eyes still
closed.
How did you know? She continues to smile.

How could I not, she answers. *Are you okay? How do you
feel, Blade?*

Right now,
I feel scared
yet full
of Joy,
is what I want to
whisper in her ear.

Yep, I'm okay.

Track 12: Right Now

ROCKERS: VAN HALEN / ALBUM: *BEST OF VAN HALEN*, VOL. 1 /
LABEL: WARNER BROS. / RECORDING DATE: MARCH 1990–APRIL
1991 / STUDIO: 5150 STUDIOS, HOLLYWOOD, CALIFORNIA

Live
the mystery

of the moment
right now.

Make a change
take a chance.

Dance today.
Grab those beats

let the rhythm
pulse through your veins.

Do what moves you
grooves you.

Right now
is what matters.

12:31 pm

When we get
to the point
where vehicles
can no longer
pass,
Elvis explains
that we will walk
a trail
then hike
a mountain,
cross three canopies,
above
the rainforest
and arrive
at the village.

He tells us
to leave behind
our failures,
broken promises,
lost love
and disappointments.

Kind of a corny script, I think,
but, when I look
at Rutherford
and Joy, I couldn't agree more.

1:30 pm

At the mountain gap
we are
a moving portrait,
carrying dirt
and stones
in our shoes,
our voices
in the echoes,
the music
in our skin,
the sounds
of our
feet thumping,
and Rutherford's
shrieks and screeches
as he starts
dancing around
like a mad man
with ants
in his pants.

HELP ME, he screams. *THERE'S SOMETHING IN MY PANTS!*

1:37 pm

There is nothing
more humbling
and probably sobering
than your father
stripping
bare naked
on a mountain
and his son
helping him brush—
with his hands—
the army
of ants crawling
all over
his unmentionables.

Conversation

These critters are buggin', Rutherford says. *Let's take a break.*
Only like three hours to go, let's keep moving, I say.

Your father's right. Let's catch our breath, Joy says,
knowing I can't refuse her.
Fine.

Blade, give your old man some of that bug spray.
Told you this wasn't a good idea.

*Of course it was. This is a big day for you. A big moment. I
had to be here.*
Yeah, okay.

At least we're spending time together.
. . . .

I thought we were cool again.
Again?

Look, I may not have been the best—
Save the "woe is me, Hollywood movie drama,"
Rutherford. I get it. You got dealt a bad hand, and you
folded.

*The drinking let me deal, but it owned me too. It was the first
thing I thought about in the morning, last thing at bedtime.*
Blame it on the alcohol.

*It helped me deal with the worst. I'm not making excuses,
it's just the game.*
It was never a game for me and Storm.

*That's not what I meant. I just want us to be cool, Blade.
I'd give anything for that.*
I hear ya. Just stay clean, and get your life together.

1:59 pm

When we resume,
Rutherford and Joy
tackle the mountain
like it's a race
to the top.

It's not a steep climb
but the heat taxes,
keeps me drenched
and even more anxious
to complete
this journey.

The trees are
old, thin giants
standing in formation
staring down
daring us to mount,
which is exactly
what Uncle Stevie attempts
before tumbling
to his feet.

Camera guy
tries his hardest
to capture all these
real moments,
but he runs
out of breath
every hundred yards,
so now Birdie films.

Travis

is his name.
He tells me
that his real passion
is making clay
animations.

*I do this filming thing to take care of my three kids and my
wife. She's in school.*
That's cool, man.

*Sorry for intruding and for the names I called you behind
your back.*

I turn to him,
hold out my hand
to say I'm sorry
because I have thought
about breaking
his nose,
and he grabs me
and hugs me like
a long-lost brother.

It's as awkward
as things can get.
But I hear grace
can feel
that way
at first.

2:19 pm

I slip
like an idiot
and cut my leg
on a rock.

Rutherford suggests
someone should pee
on my wound
so it doesn't infect.

Tell 'em, Birdie, it's medicine, right?
Not yours, Uncle Stevie says, laughing.

But Joy has something. *I brought it just in case. It's good*
medicine, she says.
Some good ole Ghana roots and herbs? Rutherford asks.

Actually, it's Neosporin.

She rubs it on my leg,
and we all laugh,
even the guide.

We're almost there I think, she says. *Twenty more minutes*
and then we tackle the last thirty meters.

2:22 pm

She could
wipe air
and pretend magic
on my wound.
It wouldn't matter,
because she is medicine.

2:43 pm

We reach the top
amidst
a million degrees
of humidity
and are given
the gift
of the most
magnificent view
any of us
have ever seen.

Golden rays streaming
over us,
as waterfalls
below
fill our eyes,

the canopies
within
our reach.

2:51 pm

I have had two
panic attacks
in my life.

One, when I was twelve
and was left backstage
in Detroit
while the band
cruised down Interstate 75.

Then, at sixteen, when I
accidently drove
down a parade route
to escape paparazzi.

But, today I refuse to give in
to the acrophobia
or to any other fear.
So, I don't look down.
But, everyone sees.

*Come on, don't let your old man show you up in front of
your girl*, Rutherford, who has smoked up a million acres
of tobacco leaves, says, making his way across canopy
one.

Uncle Stevie and Travis
nudge each other
like they're teammates
in some Hollywood
feel-good sports flick.

There are only three canopies, you will be fine, Joy says,
and I trust her, more than I've trusted anyone in this
world, including myself.
Let me just take a moment, or an hour, to catch my

breath, I answer, knowing full well that I'm at the crossroads, and on the other side of this path is my mother.

But it's too late,
she's pushing me
ahead of her,
onto this thing
that feels
more like a bunch
of quilted blankets,
any one of which
could unravel
at any second.

I close my eyes
let her hold
me around
my waist
and walk
the path
that's been chosen
for me
never looking down
or back.

3:02 pm

I make it.

We make it.

I stand
on the other side
of three bridges.
On the other side
of the mountain.

I take off
my soaked shirt
see the vast horizon
with eyes
that have never been
so open.

I'm here.
At the top
of the moment
I think
I've been dreaming about
for a long, long time.

I think of Mom,
I think of Lucy
and close my eyes,
almost unable to form
the words.
I say it,
wishing
they could both hear me.

Thank you.

Rutherford's Moment

Rutherford stands
on the edge
of the rainforest.

For a man who always had
PARENTAL ADVISORY EXPLICIT CONTENT
plastered on all his records,
this is what he shouts:

*Maybe there is a God. He probably doesn't like me much,
but he's got my respect, that's for damn sure!*

Watching Joy

She's as quiet as the clouds,
as wise as the mountain,
and as stellar as the sunrise,

and then she bows down
and speaks.

Everything is silent.
The fauna.
The birds.
The insects.

Everyone listens.

Joy's Prayer

We are closer
than we've ever been
to the sun
to a star
a real star.

Light years away,
and yet illuminating
this very day—
our lives bearing
the mortal umbra
to be filled with
merciful light.

They say
we're made
of stardust;
that would mean
we're made of
eternal light.

I think
mountain rock
and heaven's breath
too.
Amen.

Revelation

We are the sum
of moving parts
and adjustable hearts.

4:09 pm

I lead the pack
out of the rainforest
North, less than five kilometers, Elvis says.

Rutherford grabs me
from behind,
spins me around.

*This is it. The last few miles of us. You'll be changed after
this, kid.*

Maybe this is the end
and the beginning, I think.
The true beginning of all of us.

He puts his arm around me.
His guitar hits my head.

Why'd you bring that? I ask him.
You can never get lost with the music, Uncle Stevie, says,
proving that he does actually make sense sometimes.

Let's do this, I yell,
and take off running
toward
the beginning.

Turn off the camera

Rutherford says, putting
his hands
in front of the lens.

This is about Blade.
Not about me.
This is what he's come for.

Let's respect that, he says,
almost as if he's
reminding himself.

5:25 pm

Eight and a half hours later
we arrive
in a village
with colorful homes
made of mud
covered in straw
like life-sized works of art
I've seen in museums
back home.

Children in matching
red-and-orange uniforms
prance along the street
beside a skinny cow
and an even skinnier goat.

When they see us,
they stop. Joy waves.
A few return
the greeting.
Then they run.

A lone man
rides past us
on a rusty bicycle.
Akwaaba, he yells,
smiling.

We keep walking
toward
what looks like
a storefront,
where three women
sit, holding babies
and talking.

The sign out front
says:
Konko Health Post.

Joy speaks to them
in her native tongue,
and they talk back.
One of them gets up,
goes into the clinic,
and Joy's eyes reveal
a truth
I've been waiting for,
but not sure
I'm ready for.

She's here, Blade.

The Peak

Ever been
at the peak
of a grand mountain
where you can touch
the clouds
feel them moving
through you
bending sprightly
toward
the horizon
and you are overcome
unbound
and nearly
engulfed?

That is how I feel
When I see . . .

My mother

walks like
an angel,
literally;
her wings
are four girls—two
on each side—in
matching skirts
and tops.

She is short—not
much bigger
than the tweens
beside her—sporting
jeans
and sunglasses
that hide
her from me.

She drops
her glasses
and their hands
and runs
past small dwellings
past shadows
of inquisitive eyes
painted by African sun
toward
me.

She runs

down the red clay road
as if parting
the sea
to see me
to save me.

For a moment
there is no one else
but us.
Her eyes say
she knows instantly.

My whole heart pounds.
I try to force
my stiff legs
to move.
To take those
monumental steps
and walk to her.

But my feet
are fixed in concrete,
while my body shakes
like a tree
in the gale.

Can this be? she asks to no one
and everyone.

Lucy, Rutherford says, with a wide, honest grin, and
measured voice. *November.*

She looks,
remembers him,
shakes her head,
smiles, starts laughing,

and right before
running to me,
screams:

I DECLARE!

Belonging

Her embrace
is wrapped
in wild orange

with a strength
that defies
her tiny stature.

The release
of her warm tears
melts my fear.

I am locked in time,
finally hugging
the mother

I never knew
existed,
the first woman

to hold me,
to see my face,
to feel the music

strumming
in my blood.

This is where
I've needed
and wanted to be,

yet, it is a strange
and confusing place
to be told you now belong to,

like someone saying
you are from Jupiter
here's your space suit,

now take off.

Fade to Black

I hear her
say something,
but have trouble
making out
the words,
because my brain
is speeding again
running fast
running past
sunsets and
spiders
and if I could just
catch up
to my thoughts,
wrestle them
to the ground,
tame them inside
the cage
of my head,
I could breathe.
I could breathe.
Again.

Hi, is all I can manage to get out.

There is buzzing
in my ears,
numbing
in my face,
and everything slows way down,
like a show
ending
like curtains
closing

and the lights
fade
out . . .

Don't Be Afraid

On the ground,
looking up,
I see them all
staring down at me
through streams
of light.

He's not dead. Woohoo! Uncle Stevie hollers.

Someone covers my forehead
with cool hands.

Bring him inside, someone says.
He's made of rough . . . his old . . . right, Blade? someone
else says.

*Be strong, Blade. You have come this far. Don't be afraid of
the answers,* another
whispers in my ear.

I'm not scared, I say,
but the words
have no volume,
and then the curtain closes
again.

Conversation

You've come a long way just to sleep, Blade Morrison.
Where am I?

A long way from the Hotel California.
. . . .

It's nice to meet you?
You're—

Lucy November? Yes.
You're young.

Well, aren't you charming. Sunny did a good job with you. I declare!
. . . .

You probably have ninety-nine questions.
Yeah.

Let me get you some tea, and then we'll dive in.
I think I'm hungry too.

I bet you are after sleeping for a day and a half.
What? I slept that long?

You did. You woke up once when your Joy came in. She's a nice girl.
. . . .

She held your hand and sang to you.
Really?

And then you had a nightmare.
Sorry about that.

No worries, but you'll have to tell me about this spider trying to kill you.
. . . .

Sweet bread. Fruit. Hot Tea.

I smell
the peppermint tea
before she brings it in.

She sits by my side,
feeds me a spoon
at a time.

The pineapple
and watermelon
are almost as sweet
as her scent.

She runs her fingers
through my hair, then
announces the plan:

We ask each other questions, until there are no more
questions to ask.
How will that help?

A Bird Doesn't Sing Because It Has an Answer, It Sings
Because It Has a Song.
Huh?

. . . .

Questions

How does it feel to be eighteen?
How'd you know?

I was there, remember?
. . . .

How was graduation?
What do you know about Rutherford Morrison?

Oh no, did something happen?
Can we not spend our time talking about that?

How else will I get to know you, get to know all of you?
You ever seen *Star Wars*?

Who hasn't?
Can you believe he never took me to a movie? What does
that tell you?

*I'm pretty sure your father loves you, despite his flaws,
right?*
I'm pretty sure Darth Vader loved Luke also, right?

If he's so bad, how did you end up so fine?
Why does loving someone have to be so hard?

I'm impressed—have you played this game before?
Have you considered that it's not a game to me?

Blade, do you hate me?
Do you really want to know?

Do you know I love you?
Then, why you'd you give me away?

You think I had a choice?
So, you didn't?

What do you think it's like to be fifteen and pregnant?
You were fifteen?

With your whole life ahead of you?
So you chose your life over mine?

Didn't Sunny and Rutherford give you a life?
Why can't you answer my question? Why'd you give me away?

If I told you my parents made that decision, would it matter?
. . . .

. . . .
Who was my father?

Should a woman marry a man with smaller feet?
Huh?

The mood could be lightened a bit, no?
You think this is funny?

Would you rather we cry than laugh?
What do you mean?

What do you think I mean?
Was he a bad man?

What if this part of your story is tragedy—do you still want to know?
Is he dead?

Can't you see I really don't want to speak of him?
Why?

Why does evil try to collapse our hearts?
Because good is fleeting?

Is that a question?
Maybe I don't wanna know right now, okay?

So, have you found a little of what you hoped for here?
It's a start, right?

Will you stay in Ghana for a while?
Do you want me to?

. . . .
. . . .

Will you be up for meeting my friends tomorrow?
Will there be more pineapple?

I hope you'll understand that after we break bread, you must go back down the mountain, leave in the afternoon, because getting stuck here during rainy season is a horrid experience, all right?
Why, what happens?

Ever been in a landslide?
Metaphorically speaking?

You get your wit from your mother, you know that?
How do you know that?

You didn't know we grew up together?
How would I?

She didn't tell you?
She died, remember?

. . . .
. . . .

. . . .
Is it safe for you up here during the storms?

Awww, you're worried about your . . . mother?
When will I see you, when can we talk again?

How about I take you to the museums, the markets, and show you around Ghana?

Have you been to the slave castle?

Is that a place you'd like to see?
Is it painful?

We'll resume this discussion and our reunion in, say, three
days, under the big coconut tree?
That depends—do you mind a camera in your face and
our little Princess Sia climbing on my head?

Will you give her twenty hugs and kisses for me?
And winks?

Ahhh, you've given me a smile and a forever dream to build
a new world on, Blade Morrison.
That was not a question, so I guess I win the game.

What I've won today, more than makes up for the loss.

Dream Variation: Awakening

I fall out
of consciousness
into a deep,
unwavering sleep
again.

The spider
returns,
but this time
there are no
cookies
or cupcakes,
just pineapples
and Sunny
and Lucy
telling me:

Blade, wake up, turn around.
Wake Up, Turn Around.
TURN AROUND,
BLADE.

A New Day

Wake up, sport! It's back down the mountain day,
Rutherford says, so close to my face, I can smell his
breath, untainted for the first time in years. Standing
next to him is my mother.
You were dreaming about that spider again, she says.

*You remember that book you used to love when you were a
kid?* he asks.
Charlotte's Web?

*No the other one you made Sunny and I read to you every
night. You stopped reading it when she—*
I don't remember.

Was it Anansi the Spider? Lucy says.
*That was it, Lucy. We even made up songs about that
dayum spider.*

*In Ghana folklore, Anansi carries knowledge and stories to
help us triumph over challenges.*
*Come to think of it, Blade, that's when we knew you were
gonna be a rocker.*

You've been dreaming up your childhood, my dear, Lucy
says. *Remembering the gift you have. Your father tells
me you are a natural storyteller, that you weave powerful
songs.*
You said that, Dad?

Yeah, he said it, Uncle Stevie hollers. *Back from the dead,
eh?*
Birdie, get this rebirth on camera. Get us hugging, Dad
says, and she does just that,
and it's not all that bad
to be
in the spotlight
anymore.

We've missed you, Mr. Blade, Joy says, kissing me on the cheek.

At the top
of a mountain
across a rainforest
in the middle
of the bush
it seems
I have figured out
the dream
and discovered
that what I've been
searching for
has been inside
of me
this whole time.

We walk outside

where the sun blinds
and cures
at the same time.

I wave at the children
and still feel like
I'm floating
through a web
of dreams,
pulling strands
of spider silk
away from the past,
so I can step into
the here
the now.

Conspiracy

A Ghanaian bon voyage feast
has been prepared
to nurture our spirits
before the long
journey back.

After the meal
Joy says, with devious smile,
Perhaps you should play something for us, Blade.
I don't have my guitar, I hit back, swiftly.

Use mine, Dad says, high fiving Joy and handing me his
Custom-Polished-Finish Godin, which no one has ever
played but him.
Yes, won't you play a song for me, Blade? Lucy says,
knowing she's won the second she asked.

*Whatchu know about that 5th Avenue Archtop, kid? That's
a vintage guitar right there,* Uncle Stevie shouts at me.
Watch and learn, old man, I shoot back,
readying myself
to play
the biggest concert
of my life.

Track 13: Landslide

ROCKERS: FLEETWOOD MAC / ALBUM: *FLEETWOOD MAC* / LABEL:
REPRISE / RECORDING DATE: JANUARY 1975 / STUDIO: SOUND CITY
STUDIOS, VAN NUYS, CALIFORNIA.

Stevie Nicks was tired.
In her twenties
with a mountain
of woes
and a notebook
filled with music
to help
her climb
out of it.

Hmmm, sounds familiar.

Unsure
if she should continue
as a musician
or go back to school,
she gave herself
six months,
six more months
to find her song.

She went to Aspen,
and with great mountains
surrounding her,
she wrote a song
that became a classic.

And so did she.
And so did her band.

I think I have found
my Aspen,

my great mountain,
yet a part of me
is still afraid
to climb
to face myself.

I'm still afraid.
to read
The Letter
like the words
themselves
will cause
a landslide
of emotion
that will bury me
alive.

What if it's too much?
What if I let them—her—down?
What if I can't survive the landslide
of love
that I've found
all around me?

Lucy walks us to the path

we hug goodbye
for a long, long time.

*I declare, it's a weird life, Blade, when your deepest prayers
and hopes are fulfilled*, she
says.

She is everything
I never expected her to be.
And hoped she could be.
And prayed she would be.

Thank you, Lucy November, I say, not wanting to let go.
I love you, is what I want to add, so I do.

Home

The walk through
the forest
and down from
the mountain's summit

is uneventful
and filled
with silence
and happiness.

The bus
takes us back
to the place
we all call home.

We are met
by children and adults
who cannot hide
their emotions.

We think
they will celebrate
our return with feast
and dance all evening.

But it's not
a celebration that's
on their minds . . .

Chaos

There is so much commotion.
So many people shouting
at Joy
we don't know
where to run
who to see
what to do.

It's Sia, she says to us. *She is sick. We must go.*
Where, where is she?

We dash
to the local hospital,
a thirty-minute drive,
and suddenly
the rainforest
the pineapple
the familial reunion
seem far, far away
and a much easier trek
than this.

Diagnosis

Rutherford says he'll pay the world to save her.
But money can't buy everything.

Why did you tell me she was okay? he yells at Joy.
We did not know how serious it was, she answers, between
sobs.

IT'S MALARIA, HOW COULD YOU NOT KNOW? he
continues.
Dad, you don't need to scream at her. She's scared too.
We all are.

What are they doing for her? he asks, somewhat cooler.
We are treating the malaria with medication, the nurse
says.

This lethal word
is like an arrow
aimed at chest,
cutting through skin
and bone, piercing
heart
and soul.

The mosquito

is an invisible murderer,
piercing possibility
sucking futures
with its six-sworded
proboscis.

It knows just
where to bite,
which vessels
to attack,

and it shows
no mercy.
It won't even spare
the children.

What Matters

Rutherford sits
on the edge
of Sia's bed,
holding her hand.
He's humming *twinkle, twinkle,*
trying to soothe her
aches and pains.

I know I could get her the best care back at home. I'm
going to adopt her, Blade. Bring her home with me.
I don't think it's that easy, Dad.

I don't care how much it costs.

I watch him
try to get her
to eat a little,
to drink a little,
to laugh a little,
to live
a little
longer.

Unlikely, but True

Rutherford holds Sia,
tells her stories
like a father to a child.

She looks up at his face.
You can tell
a smile wants
to find its way
out.

Strange,
even in the most unlikely
of faces you can find
love.

Sia is sitting up

taking broth,
baby-sized spoonfuls.

She tugs
on Rutherford's hair;
he leans
into her
and whispers
something
I can't hear.

She grabs my hand,
her little fingers
pull mine
like they're triggers
shooting love,
and with scratchy throat
says, *Uncle, Game!*

So we play I Spy.

I spy something brown and round, I begin.
She points to my eyes.
Then Rutherford's.
Then hers,
as if we've all
come from
the same line
of tired,
worried browns.

She smiles at us
and musters
a beautiful wink.
Our Sia is coming back.
And that warms
my doubtful gut.

In a voice

that carries
love, care,
protection
and all the things
a father should bring
to the world,
Rutherford says

*You guys don't need to stay. I'll be here with her. I'll keep
her smiling. Go on, take the bus, back to the village. Get
some rest.*
What about you?

*Ah, you know rock stars don't sleep anyway. Plus, I got
Birdie and Stevie here to talk trash with while we wait this
out. Don't you two worry. She's gonna be fine. I promise
you that.*
Take Travis too, Uncle Stevie hollers. *Poor chap hasn't
been the same since the climb.*

He hugs me,
and, for once,
it feels right
and good
to hug him back.

Oh, one more thing, he adds. *That favor you wanted, it's
been delivered.*
No way, how'd you do that?

I'm a rock star, I can do whatever I want.
Where'd they put it?

The school.
So cool, Dad. Thanks.

No, thank you, son.
For what?

For giving me a reason to be better. For you.
I'll see you when you get back.

It'll be soon. Gotta make sure the dormitory gets started
before I bail. I love you, Blade.
C'mon, don't get all mushy. Let the kid go, Rutherford,
Uncle Stevie shouts.

Joy and I leave
the hospital
relieved
that Rutherford
is keeping
the night watch
over Sia.

Tuesday, 2:30 am

When we get back
to the village,
there are no drums
no dancing children
no soccer balls
no Fela
no men cutting
no women washing
and laughing
at the day's
happenings,
just me
and a river
of Joy
bathing
beneath
the African night.

Let us sit, she says,

so we do,
under the coconut tree.
She holds my hands.

You have finally met your mother. How do you feel?
Full. Happy for once.

That makes me happy, my friend.
Is that what we are, friends?

*That is the best we can be. It is the beginning of all things
that really matter.*
How do you do that?

Do what?
Make everything sound so *dayum* good.

I have a request.
Anything.

*The song you sang for Auntie Lucy was a treasure. Did
you write that?*
I wish. It's a famous American rock song.

Maybe one day, you will write a song—
For you?

For all of us, for Konko, she says, letting my hand go.
Why do you hold my hand?

Do not read anything into it, Blade Morrison. It simply
makes me feel good. Like a—
Natural woman?

Now, that is the kind of song you can write for me.
Maybe one day, I will.

Track 14: (You Make Me Feel Like) A Natural Woman

ROCKER: ARETHA FRANKLIN / ALBUM: *LADY SOUL* / LABEL: ATLANTIC RECORDS / RECORDING DATE: FEBRUARY–DECEMBER 1967 / STUDIOS: ATLANTIC STUDIOS IN NEW YORK CITY

Some people say
it's spiritual,
the relationship
between
a woman
and her God.

Some people say
it's about
how real love
makes you
feel
after you've been
rescued
from yourself
despite yourself.
When the right person
comes along
after a long, hard rain.

Funny thing is,
her producer, Jerry Wexler,
was driving down
the street
one day
contemplating
a song idea
about the natural man
when he passed by

the amazing songwriter,
Carole King.
Word is,
he shouted
I need a
"natural woman"
song
for Aretha Franklin,
and the rest
is platinum
history.

Sometimes
Fate
Is
Just
That
Simple.

Sleepy Serenade

She dozes off
right there.
So I carry her
onto the bus,
place her
in one of the bunks,
shoot a quick text to Storm
to let her know
we're both okay,
and then take
the last step
of my journey
before the roosters
and the morning taxis
bring in
the new day.

I read the letter.

Dear Blade

As I sit and write this, I look over at your blue-black eyes and copper smile. You are the happiest seven-year-old I've ever seen. You're reading comics and practicing guitar with your dad. And, I'm sad. I'm sad, because if you're reading this, it means I'm gone.

I know you'll wonder why we never told you your story before now. Blade, sometimes it's difficult to explain family and secrets and why you want to keep some things sacred and sealed until the right time. Perhaps there will never be a right time, or maybe right now it is just when you'll need to read this.

I love you, son. Your father loves you. I don't know how we got so lucky to find you, or maybe you found us. What I do know is that we were meant to be a family. We may have adopted you when you were just born, but you came to me in a dream, almost a year earlier. I remember your face. I remember your big, curly hair. I remember every second of our journey together.

Lucy November was just a girl. I used to babysit her. She never wanted to watch TV or play games, she was always reading *National Geographic*, talking about how she wanted to see the world. Save the world. I bet, if you go looking for her, and you find her, Blade, she's off somewhere changing the world.

You must know she didn't want to give you up. She had some bad things happen to her, and it scarred her. And it scared her parents. I think they thought they were doing the best thing for her by giving you a fresh start. I never worried that she'd survive though. Lucy was smart and funny, and even after everything that happened, she never lost her laugh.

When you meet her, and I'm sure you will one day, you will see it written all over her face. You will hear it in her Louisiana twang. When you do go looking, I want you to have your guitar with you. Play something special for her, Blade. I promised her you'd be okay. Show her that you are.

Forgive us, beautiful boy made of strings and frets, soundboard and a bridge, and turning pegs and chords. You are made of pure music and soul and love. And, you will always be a Morrison.

Rock and Roll, Baby,

Mom

Conversation

You've been up all night?
How can you tell?

Your eyes are blood red.
Something like that.

Your American pillows are too soft, she says, stretching her neck. *What time is it?*
About ten.

Oh my, I need to go.
First, can I show you something?

Is it coffee?
It's a surprise.

Well, it will have to wait. I cannot be late for school. I already missed three days.
It is at the school, so you will not be late.

Very well. Let me freshen myself up. Please leave the bus first. It will not look good if we walk off together.
I was a gentleman. Nothing happened.

People's minds prefer the worst.
True. I'll see you at the school. Towels are in the drawer beneath the bed.

Oooh! A shower. Nice!

Surprise

Pretty much
the entire village
is gathered
at the school,
marveling
at the glistening
white machine
at the front
of the room.

When Joy
walks through
the door,
I shush
everyone
and present
her with

A washing machine? Blade, Blade, BLADE! This is a
washing machine. Why would you do this?
Why would I not?

The entire village
applauds
and Joy
buries her head
in my chest,
her eyes
warm and
full of gratitude.

This is what friends do, I say. My father will get the
plumbing for it, but it should last for a while.
She kisses me,

and my whole world is her
right now.

The celebration
continues
outside
with each
of the women
in the village
hugging me
and thanking
my family
for our kindness.

After I hug
number nineteen,
I find Joy
and ask her
if she will
go to Accra
with me
for a proper date.

*You think because you buy a girl a washing machine that
she will have a date with you?*
I bought this for the village, not just for you, my friend, I
say almost sarcastically.

Hmmm. You make a good point, Blade.
. . . .

Are you happy?
. . . .

Blade.
. . . .

Blade, where are you going?
My father. My father's back.

Walking up the hill

is Rutherford
with shoulders slumped
and head hung low,
Uncle Stevie
toting the guitar
over his shoulder,
and Birdie trailing
not too far behind.

As Rutherford gets closer
I know.
It's all over
his face
just like before
when I was ten.

My heart dives
into to my stomach,
stops for a second
then starts swimming
so hard, so fast.
I run to him.

I don't want him
to say it.
I want him
to swallow
the news,
take us back
to yesterday
when it didn't exist,
before there was
this drowning.

The worst weapon
unleashed
on a person
are the words,
those unforgiving
words, heavy
with loss.

She's gone, he cries.

WHY?

We'll never know.
No one can ever
explain a tragedy.
We can only
write about it.
Sing about it.
Dance with it.
Move through it.

He throws
fists to the clouds.
Swearing away
any good
he ever intended.
Yelling
at anybody
everybody.

Then he grabs
his guitar
and starts
playing,
walking through
the street
like he's shredding
the place
between
heaven
and earth.
Like he's speed-riffing
a conversation
with God.

His strings
are wild horses
running
with emotions,
through time
and space.

The villagers
follow him
in awe,
join in his
testimony,
hear
his guitar
scream:
WHY WHY WHY.

The drummers appear.
The children chant.
The shekeres shake.
The people march.
The music BOOMS!

The Procession

We march,
collect more
and more
mourning passengers
as we walk
through Konko
following him,
a human train
keeping momentum
in beautiful sorrow.

We sing words
I don't understand,
but can feel
and know.

We cry with colors
that spill from our eyes,
and walk around trees,
and can't stop singing.
We won't stop singing.
The music lives.

Rutherford stops
near the well
where I first
met Joy.

He turns to face
the crowd
like he wants
to say something.
A eulogy, perhaps.
But this is not a funeral.

*A few weeks ago, a young man came to your village
searching for his soul, and you welcomed him.*
The drummers pound.

*He fell into your arms, and you held him, and I thank you,
Konko,* he continues.
The crowd cheers, *Blade, Blade, Blade!*
Then they part,
like a sea opening,
this time for me
to come
swimming through.

I shake my head,
but they won't take
no for an answer.
Their chants grow louder.
Joy pushes me
forward.

*Today, we honor Konko. We honor a thousand seasons of
your heart,* Rutherford preaches, like he's been saved.
The dancers dance
in a circle of drumming
'til they all halt
in a single BOOM!

Most of all, we honor our precious little Sia, he says,
handing me the guitar. *You know what to do.*

And, this time, I do.

Ladies and gentlemen, my son, Blade Morrison.

Solo

Precious memories
Fade like grass they say
All my memories
Of you are fresh as yesterday

I'd trade the best years of my life
For one hour of your time
But that gets tricky, I'd get greedy
And try to keep you by my side

I need you like a heart needs blood to flow
I need you like a tree needs sun to grow

All the silly, little games we used to play
A sunny life fading to gray

But I know I'm not alone again
I know I always can depend
On the times I hear
Your laughter in the wind

You promised to take care of me
And in the times I cannot see
I feel your presence here with me always

At this moment, I wish you were here
When my name is called I'd love
To feel embarrassed by your cheers

I'll still march on, holding my head high
Because of who you were and how you loved me
I know I will survive

You smiled in hard times and danced in the rain
You loved and lived so hard no one can complain
But I miss you, and I miss you

Precious memories
fade like grass they say
All our memories
Of you are fresh as yesterday

I'd trade the best years of my life
for one hour of your cries
But that gets tricky, you start winking,
I get lost inside your eyes

But I know I'm not solo again
I know I always can depend
On the times I hear
Your laughter in the wind

We promise to take care of you
But now it's time for something new
Your presence will encourage us always

You smiled in hard times and danced in the rain
You loved and lived so hard no one can complain
But we miss you, and I miss you

© BLADE MORRISON

455

I sing

for Sunny,
for precious memories

of laughter and love.
I sing for Sia,
little Blackbird

flying free.
I sing for Lucy.
Auntie. Mother. New shape of my heart.

I sing
for Storm and Joy.

For Robert,
my graduation class,
and even Chapel.

I sing for my father
and all the people
who have

given me something
to live for.
But, most of all

I sing
for myself.
The spider

I'm finally
ready
to face.

I play the song
inside
that's been waiting

for me to listen.
The one I'm finally ready
to hear.

Acknowledgments

This book is our love letter to rock and roll. We had a blast remembering the music that shaped our young lives, and writing *Solo*. We are grateful for the many people who offered encouragement along the way: Arielle Eckstut (agent and business partner extraordinaire), Annette Bourland, Londa Alderink, Sara Merritt, Liane Worthington, and Denise Froehlich (the super stellar Blink team), Jacque Alberta (wise editorial sage), Ann Marie Stephens, Sue Fliess, and Tinesha Davis (our devoted and opinionated writing "band"), Randy Preston (our awesome song and melody maker), Lezlie Evans (who brought us together), Owen Tharrington (who got his little sister hooked on KISS at age three), Mike and Becky York (our generous and patient writing retreat hosts), Juanita Britton (who introduced us to Ghana, and its beautiful people), and Emefa Ansah (who exemplifies hope). We thank our supportive families, who make sure we never have to roll solo.

Finally, thanks to YOU for checking out *Solo*. To find out more information on Kwame's literacy efforts in Ghana, visit LeapforGhana.org; to find out more about how you can help fight malaria, visit Malarianomore.org; and to listen to some of Blade's music, visit KwameAlexander.com/SoloMusicBonus.

Rock 'n' Roll, Baby!